Tell Me
Why You're Beautiful

Tell Me
Why You're Beautiful

JEREMY BROWN

ISBN: 978-1-64999-004-4   (Paperback Edition)
ISBN: 978-1-64999-005-1   (Hardcover Edition)
ISBN: 978-1-64999-003-7   (E-book Edition)

Book Ordering Information

Phone Number: 347-901-4929 or 347-901-4920
Email: info@globalsummithouse.com
Global Summit House
www.globalsummithouse.com

Printed in the United States of America

Table of Contents

Chapter 1

The emotional speech

Sitting now backstage waiting to talk to this beautiful crowd makes my heart weep and I cannot help but to remember all the circumstances that brought me here. "How ironic" I mumble to myself as I contemplate God's plans…he always knows what's best for us even if most of the time it's clear we don't understand most of it.

God's plan speaks highly of me, and His words truly uplift my soul! There are indeed people in this world who can make your day or utterly destroy your life. I consider these thoughts as the crowd gets noisier and noisier.

I cannot lie, my knees are shaking already, regardless of my experience of speaking with crowds. The feeling is the same every time. I feel connected to the people in a strange way…a way that causes me to cry while smiling. These must be tears of happiness no doubt…after all, the hard part had passed and now I had a clear path towards greatness.

There is an urge inside of me that pushes me to peek beyond the curtain, but I refrain and wait patiently as the Dean of the University speaks the magic words,

"As part of our Women Empowerment Week, we welcome one of Time Magazine's "Most Influential Women in America". She is the author of a New York Times' best-seller: 'Tell Me Why You're Beautiful', which I am sure most of you have read. Her story will change your perspective on life and I'm honored to play host to her at our University…"

His words rang like a bell in my ears and I just could not wait to get up there with all the emotions that I had gathered inside my chest.

Tina, my best friend for a long time, is with me. We have been through so much together and I just could not see my life without her. We're both fighters, we're both strong women who…now know what they want out of life and have the tools to go after it.

"Go girl…you rock!" she whispers to me smiling, "Show them how it's done!"

I can't help but smile back. She is even more enthusiastic than I am, and I can understand that. It's a huge difference between where we began and where we are now.

"Thanks, friend…no doubt, I got this" I said to her and as we hugged for a short moment.

I was not entering a competition or anything like that, but the fact that I could get up there and open people's eyes with my story meant the world to me. The fact that other girls could learn from my experiences and avoid a fate like mine was the best adrenalin rush for me. I know it might sound a bit weird, but I draw my energy from it and this helps me go on with my mission.

As I get closer to the moment when I have to step onto that stage, I stop thinking about anything else and open my mind to God for a brief moment. He had always been there for me even when I did not really see it, so I asked Hm again to give me the strength.

"Father, I thank you for watching over me as you have always done, and for giving me the energy and inspiration to reach into the hearts of these kids. Work through me…"

My prayers got interrupted suddenly by the Dean's words:

"Without further ado, please welcome Jamie!"

I suddenly open my eyes and I cannot stop a single tear from rolling down my cheek.

"It's ok, you can do it!" I say to myself as I look back at Tina.

She keeps pushing me through the air forward… making that sign "go, go" and that meant I really had to go, there was no way around it!

As I walk on stage, the audience goes crazy. People stand up clapping and cheering and I just can't stop the rosy blush that begins to fill my cheeks. The atmosphere is overwhelming as the whole room is filled with noise and cheering.

I never considered myself as a star or anything near it, yet I wanted my ideas and thoughts to reach as many people as possible… the rest of it comes with the territory, you know the saying.

For a moment there, I was awestruck and did not see anything around me…not even the Dean who was coming to shake hands with me. I know it might have seemed rude of me, but I was engulfed with all the love and appreciation.

"We're so happy to have you here!" the Dean said to me as we shake hands "I believe the kids will learn a great deal from you… you're a living inspiration."

I wanted to reply but couldn't find the proper words to say.

As soon as the 'shaking hands' moment was over, the crowd is seated and for the first time I can now see how many people are here. From the looks of it, there is not an empty seat.

"This is going to be intense," I think to myself and try to clear my throat as I know a pretty long speech is about to follow.

I take a few deep breaths because I will really want everyone in the audience to connect to my story. Looking at the people in the front row, I could see them all perfectly, it's clear to me that the kids are sipping my every gesture, my every move. It's clear to me that they are waiting for something extraordinary to come out of my mouth and this gives me the chills.

The Dean quickly adjusts the mic for me. This is not the first time I've talked in front of an audience, but I have no idea how the words will flow because I'm always caught up with emotion. This happens whenever the temperature rises in my face and whatever words follow are beyond my control.

I grab the mic but I could not tell if it was working, so I poke it a couple of times to make sure that everything is working in perfect order.

"Please don't kill it…we wanna hear your story" a student in the front row jokes and that really put a smile on my face.

"Don't worry…it's allliveee" I reply in the same tone and prepare for the serious part of my speech.

"Hello, everyone…and I'm sorry, I don't usually get this worked up. Today I can feel something special taking place so I cannot hold my emotions" I said as the whole audience listened to me in perfect silence. The students were breathing in my every word…the atmosphere was indeed intense.

I stop for a moment and take another look at that sea of people who were hoping to get inspired by my speech.

"Listen, I wanna tell you something important and I want you to pay attention to the words I'm about to utter," I said trying to make sure that everyone could hear me. They were paying attention anyway, but I just wanted to make sure that my voice was clear.

"I woke up this morning with a feeling in my heart that someone who would be here in the audience today…" I said and then stopped abruptly. All of a sudden I feel like I need to take another deep breath. The things that I am about to say, will not come easy as those memories are still somewhere buried deep in my heart.

"As I woke up, I knew I would meet someone who came here in the last act of desperation…and maybe there's more than one."

Words are flowing easier and easier out of my mouth, and I feel like some greater force is speaking for me. This is not the first time this has happened to me…after all, I often have the same experience when writing things on paper. I came here to inspire and maybe teach the students, I wasn't sure if this would be accomplished, but I could sense that God's will would be done.

As I look to my right, I can see Tina who is rocking from side to side interceding for me. Seeing her adds even more fuel to the fire that is in my spirit.

As I begin to understand where the speech is going I prepare a full disclosure. I know this is the only way I can make them understand the meaning and the reasons behind my book.

"Whether you've read my book or not, now I will tell you the reason behind the story and all the things I left out of my book. As much as I wanted to write it all down, there are still a lot of things that have been left out; some of them were too painful to share publicly."

"We are all running from pain, be it physical or psychological. No one in their right mind wants to suffer, thus we either face the pain, run away from the pain or try to bury the pain that has been inflicted upon us."

Everyone has their ears perked up while absorbing my words, and I can feel the tension building in the room…I continue.

"Hiding is never an option or trying to pretend that something isn't there…the pain will always find a way to come to the surface if we choose not to face it head on! I realized this just this morning as I woke up after having a terrible nightmare. I was reliving all those hellish memories and dark days that scared me to the depths of my soul. However, I knew instantly that this was me…it may be where I was at a point in time but it is not who I am, not the true me!"

As I look for a brief moment into the room smiling slightly, I can see the students' eyes bulged almost popping out. They are caught up completely and I have yet to disclose anything significant. The Dean is also listening carefully to my every word; he probably knows bits of my story from my book.

"My hope right now" I continue "is that after I reveal my whole self before you, the people in this room who feel the burden of desperation, will find an answer or the strength to start searching for their own answers. I hope to open your eyes toward the brighter future that awaits you. Trust me; even during the darkest moments of your life, you can find your purpose if you look in the right direction. I know I did, and I know that God helped to open my eyes towards my divine destiny…in my case, it was to help others overcome adversities."

Some of the students clap for a few brief moments, but soon enough the silence falls again over the crowd. I have a few more words to say and then I'll reveal my life story.

"The reality we live in today is pretty twisted and at times and it's complicated to discern what's true and what's not. Unexplainable things happen to us that are hard to take in, but this is life. As long as we decide to fight for our shot at greatness, I don't think there's any weapon formed that could stand in our way."

"Many say that we're all born equal in this world with equal chances, but I believe there's more, I believe that somehow, we're connected and we can help and influence each other…for better or worse. I want to point you in the right direction and show you through my experiences that each one of you has the strength to go on no matter what."

"For that reason, I will tell you the full story of my life. All the twists and turns, ups and down and all the demons I had to face. In times when kids were playing with their feet in the sand, my eyes were witnessing terrible things…dark things, and even though I could not understand the reasons why everything was happening to me…I knew that I was different!"

Chapter 2

The heartbreaking purchase

I REMEMBER THAT DAY LIKE IT WAS YESTERDAY. SOME memories you can never get rid of, regardless of how much you try.

It happened 17 years ago, and even though 17 years might sound like an eternity, it isn't! I was only 13 years old. There I was, sitting in the corner of our living room, hiding in the shadows and terrified as I watched my mother smoking meth out of a pipe.

The way my mother was enjoying that poison, knowing that it could lead to her untimely death still puzzles me to this day. She exhaled the smoke out of her mouth slowly; savoring it like it was the last day of her life.

The drug had transformed my mother; meth had turned her into some entity I could not recognize anymore. The gaze in her eyes was different, she did not behave like she used to and it looked like I had fallen off her list of priorities completely. Her only priority these days was to find a way to get another fix.

I couldn't tell anymore who my real mom was; she had these bipolar episodes with mood swings from north to south. I have to admit that I was afraid of her to some extent…I was afraid of what she had become because of that drug.

"Jamie darling…why are you hiding over there in the darkness…come to me!" she whispered and smiled with her yellowish teeth. From the tone of her voice, it appeared to me that she was afraid that someone would hear her even if we were the only ones in the room.

"I'm fine mom" I replied with my usual sad voice. How could I be happy when I was living in darkness?

"No, you're not fine…you're hiding; come here by my side" my mother insisted, but going near her was the last thing I intended to do.

"I told you I'm fine! I can't stand the smell of that stuff." I cried out, but I could not shake my mother from her calmness. She had her fix now and she could care less if my whole world was about to end… her brain was too numb to care anyway.

"Why are you talking to me like that? I am your mother." she insisted. I hated when she played that 'guilt game' with me. I knew it was not real, or at least was simply a fleeting moment of compassion for me.

"Leave me alone mom, I'm fine where I am…keep smoking your pipe and pretend I'm not here!" I replied and this triggered a 'motherly response' in her. From time to time she felt the need to state her prerogatives even if she did not really mean them…or at least that's what I felt.

"I don't like you staying in the dark…I need you to come by my side, so I can protect you. You're my baby, I need to protect you!" She insisted, but I was not going to leave my place. My heart was dark already so I might as well sit in the darkness for the rest of my life.

At times, during her drug induced mood swings, my mother would cry and blame herself for all kinds of things. I guess her subconscious was coming up to the surface engulfing her in guilt and remorse… was it real or just a twisted act? I couldn't really tell.

As we were arguing, me in the dark and my mother high on meth, I heard a door slam against the wall. Luckily I was not too close, otherwise, the door would have hit me.

"Where the heck is my pipe…I'm going crazy looking for it!" my father shouted, but my mother could care less. She was too stoned to understand the question and simply laughed at my father who was a ball of nerves.

"I have nooo ideaaa" My mom replied, but she had used it to smoke meth just seconds prior to my father entering the room.

"For god's sake…a man can't find nothing in this house!" he yelled again but my mother was oblivious…she kept on with her pointless laughing driving my father to his wit's end.

"You know Dorothy…if you would keep this house in order I's be able to find my pipe without turning everything upside down," he added with an irritated posture. My mother kept smiling at him for no apparent reason and this caused him to react.

"Why are you smiling anyway…what's so funny about you not doing anything useful around this house?"

"I fouundd your pipee" my mother teased as if she was a little girl. "You want it?"

"I was looking for it, wasn't I? Where the heck is it?"

In that moment, my mother picked up the pipe she had just smoked from; it was right behind her back, but she acted like that was the first time she had seen it all day.

My father quickly snatched the pipe from her and lights it hoping there was something left, but the meth was kicked. I wish I could find the words to depict the disappointment in his eyes; his face looked like his own child had died or something.

"This smoke is done…for god's sake! Did you smoke all of it woman?"

My mother kept laughing slowly as if she was trying to drive him nuts on purpose.

With no meth in his system, my father quickly started losing his temper and with each failed reply from my mother, he was closer to slapping the meth out of her. This would not be the first time when things ended in violence between them.

"Did you forget about me or something?" my father asked for the last time and right before my mother could nod her head, he slaps her across the face.

She was not scared at all…it looked like she was enjoying it. I, on the other hand was terrified. I flinched into the corner and covered my head with both my hands. I did not want to hear or see anything and I wished I could just disappear.

My mother's nose was bleeding and she had blood through her yellow teeth too, but she did not seem to care about it as she continued to smile. She licked her teeth clean with her tongue and started laughing hysterically…

"You really hit like a woman Bill…I always thought you were the strong type but it looks like I had been wrong this whole time," my mom replied and tried to jump on his back.

My father was not into playing games and pushed her away…

"Ohh God, how much I want to wipe that smirk off your face" he shook with anger "You are worthless…you know that? And now you smoked all of our stuff!"

It was clear to me that things were not going to end there. Every time my father started grinding his teeth, it was a sign that something terrible was about to happen and I was right this time as well.

Before I could even think of something to do, my father grabbed my mother's hair with all his strength and pulled her towards him. This almost caused her to fall if it was not for my father's body.

I suspected that she would scream or something because of the pain, but my mother did not say a word and looked like she was enjoying this masochistic act.

"That was the last of it, am I right?" My father growled at her as my mom was sitting in an unnatural position with her neck bent all the way towards her spine and barely standing on her toes.

"Sorry, but there's none left…I smoked it all up!" she replied trying not to lose her breath.

My father yelled at the top of his lungs and pushed her against the wall releasing his grip.

My mother hit the wall like a bullet, and still, she made no sound. This twisted ballet they were dancing was freaking me out because I did not understand if they were for real or if that was just their way of handling each other.

"You'll be fine, don't worry" my mom replied a few moments later after she got up and straightened her hair like a diva. Her reckless behavior was confusing me.

"Ohh no no no… get up and get me what I need…tonight! Or else…" my father added. The look on my mother's face was as if she was waiting to see what followed after that 'or else' since my father was wearing a classic smirk on his face.

"Or else…what? You think you're scaring me boiiii?" she yelled at my father who was about to leave the room, but he turned around now that she was challenging him.

"What did you say to me?" he said looking at her with his left eyebrow up. "You smoke every ounce and now you think you're tough? Ohh let me show you what tough really means…and then we'll talk about it!"

My mother did not care at all that his anger was through the roof by now; she threw herself onto the sofa and pushed her hand through her hair.

"Have you turned into Mr. Monopoly all of a sudden without telling me? What's with this sudden shift in your behavior?"

My father could not believe her boldness, and I could not tell if he was going to hit her again. It was clear by now that my mother could take quite a few hits and still be the same…thus she took the fun out of it for him.

"What are you talking about woman? Have the drugs screwed up your brain that bad? Are you out of your mind or something?"

"You know…money bags? that stuff" she said and smiled at him.

"That stuff, you were supposed to get two nights ago…but nahh, you kept your lazy behind inside smoking what I brought. Living the good life right…bravo, you're quite the heroine!" he said sarcastically.

Hearing my father's words, my mom's face changed in a split of a second. She put on that serious mask you'd see on a business woman, or any respectable person who knows what they want from life.

"Darling, from what I remember, we were a team and this means we have to work together and not accuse each other for things that are in the past!"

My father gasped heavily "Ohh and where's your contribution partner? Where's her contribution? From what I recall, only I struggle to bring something in, while you two sit around all day long and do nothing!"

All of a sudden, I found myself involved in their fight even if I had not said a single word during the whole scene. I was there and this was probably enough for them to hold me accountable.

"Did you bring anything in?" he said looking at me with his clouded eyes.

I was afraid that he would hit me too even if I had nothing to do with their drugs. Too many times I had been a collateral victim and I knew quite well the roughness of his hands…most of the times for no apparent reason and at no fault of mine. To me, it felt like I was guilty for just being born into this family.

I nodded and whispered "no".

My father's nerves were stretched to their limit and he did not care anymore that I was still a child.

"Speak up…I can't hear a word your saying" he yelled at me and I just couldn't help it and I started crying.

"I don't have any money…I have not gone out this week" I replied and I could see that was the wrong answer.

"You haven't?" he looked at me with a grimace on his face "Whoa whoa…what do you mean? Were you sick or something?"

"No I'm fine…I just did not feel like going…" I said in a way that was not supposed to upset him, but there was no way around his anger.

"You did not feel like it, huh?" he said grazing his beard with his right hand.

It was clear that he wanted to beat the light out of me, right there, right then, but I got lucky for some reason…at least for a brief moment.

"Dorothy…did you hear what your beloved daughter just said to me?" he yelled at my mother who was still lying on the couch.

"Stop yelling like a mad man… I can hear you, can't you see that I'm only two feet away?" mom replied in a shallow attempt to jump in my defense, but I knew this would not last very long.

"Did you hear her?" My father insisted and this time, my mom came to me and tried to wrap her arms around me... like a good mother.

"Don't worry baby, everything is going to be ok" she said to me but I did not believe a single word.

Meanwhile my father looked at us with pity in his eyes and also anger. All he cared about was the money and he would not hesitate for a second to throw me out into the street if I did not bring him anything...and the same rule applied for my mother.

"She said she did not feel like going out...can you believe this!" and this is how my father started yet another of his monologues. I never dared to interrupt him because I knew what would follow if I did.

"Well that's not the answer I wanna hear coming from that pretty mouth of yours...and you know why? I am sick of being the only fool around here who busts his butt trying to make some cash...while you just sit around here smoking up everything and laughing about it!"

Unfortunately, there was no laughing involved...at least not for me. I drowned in tears so often that at times I forgot why exactly I was crying.

He saw the tears rolling down my face, but he did not flinch; and he was not done by any means.

"So, since we all know that your mother will not do anything about it... just look at her, she's a train wreck...this means that it's your turn baby girl to step up and make a quick buck for us. You see how bad we are struggling right?" he said and I just wanted to say something in my defense...I wanted to convince him...

"Daddy please...I don't want to do this anymore...pleaseee!"

His ears were shut and I could never reach him even if I was standing in front of him with tears.

"I don't wanna see no tears...I want to see you out there making some cash, that's what I want! So stop whining about it and act like a woman; you're a woman now...you're not a little girl anymore!" and yet I was only 13 when this episode was taking place.

I pushed my mom away. She was not helping me. All I wanted back then was to jump in front of a train and make it all go away. I felt I could not take it anymore…but something just wouldn't let me take my own life.

I crawled back in my dark corner and waited for all to end… unfortunately, my father's show had only started.

"And since I am the only one who worked this week, it means that somebody is going to suffer in the next few days, and that sure as heck ain't gonna be me!" he said cunningly and his words made my mother perk up. She knew exactly what he meant.

"Bill don't…" she tried to say but he stopped her short.

"Yeahh…you got that right! I am buying this week alright, but you ain't seeing a bit of it, that's right!" he laughed in her face.

My mother's drug addiction was so bad that if she did not have her fix at the right time, she would go crazy and her body would shut down in ways words can hardly describe. She barely survived the last 'shortage' of drugs and my father remembered that all too well.

"Baby, you can't do that to me…you know what happened the last time" mom tried to plead with him, but his heart was out of reach.

"Ohh I know, don't worry my love…but you should know there are consequences to not going out and keeping this little one with you. So, right now, this is your problem to solve."

My mother looked at him silently and I could read the despair in her eyes. I guess he kinda felt some sort of satisfaction knowing that we would get punished for our 'disobedience'. Everything was on the line as he refused to even buy the necessities, like food and clothing, if we did not go out.

"Do you have anything else to say to me… I believe we have it all cleared up" he added with the same smirk on his face. Now the table had turned and mom was the one worried and nervous.

"As for you darling" he turned his eyes towards me. I was still sitting in my corner silently. "You are going out there tonight and I don't want to hear a word about it!"

"Please daddy…don't make me do it again…I'm begging you!" I said between tears hoping I could make him reconsider but there was no compassion to be found.

"Shh…what did I tell you that I don't wanna hear a word…go get me some money."

It was futile for me to say anything in this situation, so I decided to shut my mouth.

"I told you I am in no mood for your foolishness," he added even though no one had said a single word and walked towards the door to grab a coat from the rack.

I turned my head away towards the window in sorrow. Tears were a common thing and even though they could not appease my soul anymore they still gave me some form of relief…at least for a little while.

The thought of going back on the streets, terrified me. All those past experiences and all those creepy men who looked at me as if I was a piece of cheap meat turned my stomach. I had nowhere to go, I had no one else but those two drug addicts who were willing to sell me piece by piece for a few bucks.

"Where are you going?" my mom asked as he was about to walk out the front door.

"Ahh…none of your business…out, what would you care anyway!" he replied and my mother jumped at his feet.

"Please, don't leave me like this…I'll do anything you want… just…" she begged and he looked at her the way probably Caesar looked at his defeated enemies when he had his foot on their neck.

"You don't say… be a good girl and maybe I'll let you take a hit."

When hearing those words, my mother jumped at his neck and started kissing him all over his face… "Thank you…thank you!"

"Aww get off me…" he replied and pushed her to the side "I'm in no mood for your theatrics, I have business to take care of!"

Right when I thought that I could have a little bit of silence finally, he turned his attention towards me again as he was one-foot through the door.

"I want my cash tonight" he said to me. "If I don't find it on this freaking table when I come back… you're gonna be in deep trouble!"

And…he left. I turned my head against the window and fell on my knees. I wanted to get under that window pane if that was possible…

I did not want to go out there for a single second as I felt like my soul was dying a little bit each time a stranger was laying his hands on me.

As I was sitting there in the corner sinking in my own misery, my mother approached me.

"Are you okay honey?"

"Do I look like I am okay mom? I'm not and I will never be living here with you two!" I cried out, but she wasn't really asking me because she cared about me. She rather cared about the money I would make so she could buy some more meth.

"Darling, you know you have to go right… I mean…" she tried to convince me that this was necessary when in fact it wasn't.

"Why should I know that…why should I have to put up with any of this…whyyy?" I screamed and she tried to hug me. I pushed her away… "Leave me alone!"

"You know…your father…" she added and I could feel her voice scratching on my ear drums.

"I can't do it…I just can't…kill me if you want, but I won't do it anymore…I'm only 13 for God's sake; doesn't that mean anything to you?"

Then, she looked straight into my eyes…

"Do it for me…do it for mom… I am desperate, can't you see?"

"It hurt me so much the last time…I don't think I can take it again" I cried. As I sat there as she laid her head on my shoulder as if to comfort me, it felt as though she could not hold it up on her own anymore. Seconds later, she passed out.

"Mom…mom are you ok?" I tried to bring her back but her pupils were the size of grains of sand.

"Ohh my God…oh my God…" I said to myself as I was walking back and forth through the living room. I only knew one way to help her, because I had seen it happen before and the meth would bring her back somehow. It was worse than a freak show, but that was the only way I knew.

I dragged her to the couch and tried to call my father, but he did not answer his phone. Sitting next to her for more than half an hour,

I pondered on what I should do and soon I felt the room was spinning round and round. I had cried so much it was like my body was down to the last drop of energy. Before I knew it, I fell asleep on the couch next to my mother. This was a blank sleep; my brain was too tired to dream anything and even if it did, I am sure it would have been something terrible…so it was better this way.

When I woke up it was already night outside. My heart started racing thinking that my father had already returned and I had not made any money. After I saw that he had not returned yet, I started looking for one of the outfits he bought for me so I could draw more clients.

Those clear heels along with the tiny top and 6 inch skirt made me look like a true lady of the night. When you hear people say that clothes don't make a man or a woman…well, that's not all true, clothes do say a lot about a person and I learned that the hard way.

The bright colors of my clothes made me look like a peacock who was eager to mate. As I was staring in the mirror I wanted to just smash my head against it and forget all about it…hmm how simple this would make everything right?

My father had told me where to go, he even took me to the spot the first time I went to the street corner. Well, he kinda dragged me over there in front of all the other girls who were hoping for a quick buck and felt no remorse at all.

This time, I was going on my own. With my knees shaking as I was leaving the house and hoping in my mind that I would come back alive. You never know what psycho you might find out there and what twisted thoughts they have in mind. Being a lady of the night is probably one of the most dangerous 'jobs' in the world especially when you are young and inexperienced.

As I reached the street corner under the bridge, I started getting cold. The weather was pleasant, but my body was shivering for some reason. Mostly because I was afraid of what was going to happen next…I had no idea what would follow and that scared me the most.

My skirt was rising up as I was walking and I tried desperately to pull it down as much as possible but to no avail.

That street under the bridge was a common ground for street walkers, and that night the place was filled with girls and even a few young boys that were going back and forth looking to catch the big fish.

They all wore the same type of clothes…high heels, tiny skirts and t-shirts and the boys were shirtless. The fact that I found myself among them, made me feel like I was in the loneliest place on earth. Some of them were probably in my situation or even worse, but I did not think about their circumstances back then, I only focused on my own misery.

In this business you have to look sharp and make the man understand that with you, he's gonna have the time of his life. For that reason, you have to move…you have to draw them in like a magnet. I had no knowledge about any of that, so I looked around at the girls that were already there and tried to emulate their behavior.

So, I started walking down the sidewalk looking right and left at what the others were doing already; it did not take too long to see one of them, who was much older…well she was having sex right there in front of everybody and looked like she was proud of it. The whole scene was so grotesque to me that I turned my eyes away from it hoping not to have a nightmare later that night.

My skin turned to all goosebumps and I felt disgusted with myself.

"Will I end up like one of those women?" I wondered but did not have the courage to look for an answer. I just closed my eyes and took a deep breath, wishing at the same time that I would be taken out of this misery one day.

With my head down, I continued walking down that sidewalk, all of a sudden, my eyes were blinded by the shiny headlights of an approaching car. As the car slowed down I could see that it was a pristine Mercedes…quite a fancy car. I did not know if they were coming to me until the passenger window was lowered and a man stuck his head out of the car.

"Pff…this is it!" I said to myself and took a deep breath, but as I was walking slowly towards the car, another girl almost pushed me off the sidewalk…

"Move aside lil girl…let a real woman handle this man; get lost!"

I tried to keep my balance as I was not used to wearing such high heels, and looked at how she almost threw herself inside the car.

"S'up baby…you're up for some lovin' tonight" she said to the man and then stopped talking suddenly; she looked like her tongue had been cut with a knife. Her eyes widened and she took a step back.

"I'm so sorry…I did not know…please forgive me…" she apologized frantically and this made me think.

"Who is this guy?"

"Beat it" he told her and the she ran to the other side of the road.

"Now what?" I thought to myself "What if he wants to talk to me? Should I give in?"

Moments later and he waves to me.

"Hey there…little girl, come over here!" he said and I was reluctant in approaching the car now after I had witnessed that strange scene.

"What do you want?" I asked him.

He smiled back at me with the looks of a man who knows and has seen too much.

"You're curious to know?" he added and waved for me to get closer.

This time I took a few steps towards the car…what could he do to me right? After all, I had no idea who he was…

"Does the name Francisco say anything to you?" he asks and I had no idea. I mean I did not know anyone by that name…except for a boy in school, but I was sure he was not referring to that little kid.

I nodded no, and he smiled back at me…

"Nice, nice…if you don't know about it, it means you are far too young to be out here…am I right?"

I looked away trying to disguise my shame because I knew he could see it on my face that I was just a child…even through all the makeup I had put on.

"I don't know what you mean, I'm 18…" I replied still looking away.

"Ohh yeah, and I am the freaking president! Stop lying to me… and more importantly to yourself."

My hands started sweating and shaking violently but I kept them together so I could mask the fact that I was about to wet myself…

"Calm down…nobody is going to hurt you!" He said to me "I am Francisco, and even if you don't know me today, you will from now on!"

"What's your name?" he asked with a voice so kind it instantly made me want to believe everything that he was saying.

"Jamie?" I stuttered.

He looked at me, scanning me from top to bottom.

"That's a beautiful name you got" he replied while I still avoided looking straight at him.

He noticed that I was shy and scared…how could he not? He could tell so much just by looking at a woman.

"Hey…hey…look at me."

When I tried to look at him, I could feel even my eyelashes were trembling with the rest of my body. As I finally raised my eyes and looked straight into his, he poked the man who was in the car with him.

"What?" I asked confused because I had no idea exactly what he wanted from me.

"Be calm…I'm not trying to sleep with you or anything!" he said and started writing something onto a little piece of paper.

"Then what do you want with me?"

He smiled again… "Right now, I don't want anything."

"Well, if you'll excuse me, I came here for a purpose and you're kinda wasting my time right now" I replied and tried to walk away from the car.

"Yo…hold up! I did not tell you to leave. I'm not a trick, but that does not mean I cannot have a valuable conversation with you!"

I said those things because I wanted to get away, not because I really meant them. Having sex with all those sleazy men that were pulling up under that bridge was the last thing I wanted to do. So, I turned around…I kinda felt safe next to Francisco, even though I could not explain that sensation.

"What exactly do you want?" I asked him as I got closer to him.

He looked like he did not know exactly what to say…

"Ughh…don't you have parents? I mean, do they know that you are here doing this?"

I was ashamed to admit that my parents were the ones who put me in that situation, but I could not lie either! I was not going to…

"I would not be here if they did not force me to" I replied and he looked shocked to hear it. In hindsight, I think the shocked look was only to lore me in with false empathy.

"Whaaat…that's bad" he replied "but you're not the only case I have heard of over the years unfortunately."

I tried as much as I could to keep my tears inside me, but a few of them got out, so I tried to wipe them as fast as possible.

"Don't cry now…this will not solve anything for you! How about we pay them a visit huh?" he added and his tone really scared me.

I had heard all kinds of stories with thugs and pimps and I really did not want my parents to get hurt…as awful as they were. He probably saw the fear on my face, so he changed his voice a little bit.

"What do you say?"

"No, no, I don't want to get into even more trouble!" I said and walked away from the car.

"Don't worry…I'm not going to hurt them, God no! I have different plans in mind you know…I'd like to do business together, and if things work out, your parents get quite rich and pretty fast too. Don't you think they would like that?"

His words rang like a bell in my head. We had money problems since I could remember…and now this opportunity…

I had no idea what Francisco really wanted, but there was one certainty! If I did not make money for my father, he would beat me until he grew tired of doing it. I was in a situation where taking risks was a natural thing…after all, things were getting worse regardless of whether I did something or not. So I decided to take this chance and go with Francisco's idea.

"So, have you thought about it?" he says to me seeing that I was lost in my head for a few moments.

"How much money are we talking about?" I asked instinctively, but he was not going to reveal anything to me, at least not until we got home.

"Just get in the car…you'll see that I am talking real business," he said to me then leaned and opened the door for me… just like a real gentleman, wouldn't you think?

I got in that fancy Mercedes and Francisco drove back to my parents' apartment. I was scared because I had no idea what their reaction would be and I did not want the whole thing to end up in a nasty drama.

Francisco kept looking in the rear mirror as he was driving, probably trying to see how I was doing. I did not say a word as I kept thinking what to say to my father once we got there because I was sure that he would become violent, especially if he hadn't smoked yet.

When we finally got home, my hands were shaking violently as I grabbed the handle of the door and Francisco saw this.

"Don't be afraid, everything is going to be ok" he said and winked at me hoping that this would calm me, but I was far from being calm…I was preparing for the worst.

When I finally managed to open the door of the apartment that leads straight into the living room, I could not see anyone. I looked left and right but the living room was empty. Francisco quickly followed me and I closed the door behind him.

"It looks like your parents are not home right now" he said to me turning his golden ring on his pinky. "Maybe I should come another time."

I did not know how to reply…and to tell the truth, I was afraid to be alone in the house because I knew that my father would beat the living soul out of me. I did not have any money, and if Francisco left with his business proposal, that meant I had no reason to be home empty handed.

Now, after probably hearing the noise, my father came out of the bedroom already mad…and he was kinda shocked to see Francisco standing there.

"So, where is my money, huh?" he yelled at me, but I did not have any and was afraid to say so.

"And who is this Luciani looking dirtbag, who dares to look at me like that...in my house!"

I tried to explain to my father the whole situation but words would not come out of my mouth, so Francisco stepped in.

"How rude of me, let me introduce myself...I am Francisco!"

"Whatever" my father replied with a disgusted voice "save your cheesy introduction...as for you, did you think you could bring this guy and have sex with him...and for free too? You must be out of your mind!"

"I did not bring him to have sex!" I replied almost in tears "I just..." and right then Francisco put up his hand telling me to shut up.

I quickly understood the message and shut my mouth...I was not in a condition to speak anyway.

"Sir, why don't you calm down and listen to what I have to say...it won't cost you a dime, on the contrary..." Francisco replied and this caught my father's attention.

"Yeah, what's this all about?" my father mumbled with the voice of a man who does not want to admit he is wrong even if he knows he is.

"I have not come here for any sexual favors, but rather with a business proposal in mind. I'd say you should thank your daughter for inviting me here; you have no idea what an opportunity you have on your hands."

Francisco spoke with the diplomacy of a real politician even if he was a pimp...this attitude was quite attractive if we left aside the fact that he was exploiting young girls for cash...

"Shall we take a seat...so that we can discuss further?" he said to my father who was standing with his back against the wall wearing only some old shorts.

"I'm good standing...so get to your point because I don't have the all night!" my father replied with an angry voice. He was probably annoyed by Francisco's lax voice and superior attitude.

I was standing a few feet away from my father, somewhere close to the door entrance and tried my best to avoid his gaze. His eyes were searching me continuously and I could feel them piercing my insides. If Francisco was not there, I would be in a very different situation... with my body badly beaten and bruised.

Francisco kept looking around the living room studying everything that was to be studied. It was clear that he had a keen eye for details and could exploit even the smallest advantage in any situation.

"You have a nice place, I'm sure you must feel quite comfortable in here" Francisco observed with a rather sarcastic voice, but my father was not buying into his 'sincerity'.

"This is really not your business, so I suggest you cut the smooth talk and tell me exactly why you have come into my home at this time of night!" my father replied irritated "You'd better tell me how much and for what before I lose my temper and throw you and your pretty suit through the window!"

"No need for violence sir," Francisco smiled "we are both civilized men and I am sure we can conduct business together."

"Alright, what is your deal then?" father replied with a calmer voice, but Francisco was determined to teach him a lesson.

"You should never jump the gun when you clearly know you don't have the upper hand and...you should do your best to listen more than talk... you know what I am sayin'...be wise as a serpent, not stupid like a mouse, because wisdom will get you rich, while stupidity will get you more of the same!"

My father was not the man to whom you could tell what to do or teach a lesson...even now, he could hardly control himself, but I guess the idea of getting money was more important than teaching Francisco a lesson of his own.

"You're in my house, aren't you? This means I have the upper hand and I can do whatever I want..." he said and Francisco kept waving his finger through the air.

"No no...this is where you are wrong...and you should listen very carefully, you might be older but you're not that smart...at least not as smart as you think you are!"

"You no good…" my father tried to say and storm towards Francisco but he stopped in time for some reason.

Francisco turned his head and looked straight at me…

"You know, you have a very lovely daughter and she deserves much more than you are offering her right now. This so called life you are providing her is nothing compared to what she could have." Francisco argued and Bill was on the brink of throwing him out of the apartment.

"You don't know a thing about me and my family, so I suggest you choose you words carefully. It's none of your business how I live my life!"

Francisco scoffs lightly… "That's exactly what I am saying…it's her life, not yours, and you should keep in mind that Jamie has to live her life her own way, not just doing whatever you tell her to do."

Francisco did not get to finish his sentence, and my mother stumbled out of the bedroom, half naked and quite woozy. She could barely see where she was going but she remembered to ask about me.

"Has Jamie come back?" she asked Bill, and I suspect that she failed to see me and Francisco in the living room. Her eyes were too cloudy to see anything else but the smoking pipe at that time.

On the other hand, Francisco notices her mesmerizing presence immediately.

"Ohh and this must be your lovely wife…I can see where Jamie's beauty comes from" he said trying to be a gentleman.

"You should mind your own business" my father acidly replied and then turned his attention towards my mother. "Dorothy, get back inside right now!"

My mother was too confused to comprehend and felt like she had to intervene somehow. So, after measuring Francisco from top to bottom a couple of times, she looked at him with her eyebrows raised.

"And who are you now?" she said looking at Francisco who kept his mouth shut. "Honey who is this fellow? Is this the one bringing our stuff?" When seeing that she could not get an answer from my father she turned her head again towards Francisco "Do you have the drugs…give me some!"

Throughout this whole scene, Francisco kept nodding in disapproval. It was clear that any comment would be useless so he just waited for the whole thing to end naturally.

"Are you mute or something?" My mother yelled at him.

Bill could hardly keep it together.

"Dorothy, didn't I tell you to get back inside? Have you forgotten English or something?"

"But Honey, I just…" My mom replied and tried to make one-step, but she stumbled to the table and my father grabbed her strongly by her hand.

"What did I tell you about how much I hate when you interfere in my business?" he grinded his teeth and pushed her back into the bedroom where my mother fell on the floor.

I was terrified to see my father hurting her, and even though this wasn't the first time but when they treated each other like that it scared me. Bill did not care if strangers were in the house…he would do whatever he pleased whenever he wanted to.

Francisco tried to help me calm down as he saw my entire body shaking, so he came closer to me and smiled kindly.

"It's going to be ok, don't worry…leave them to their game, it's clear that they don't know otherwise!"

I did not say a thing, as I was both afraid and ashamed by my parents' behavior. They were acting like savages treating each other in the worst ways.

"Sir, I am willing to offer you ten thousand dollars, ok" he said while turning towards my father who lost his voice all of a sudden. He forgot that he was yelling at my mother and his eyes widened like never before.

"Ten thousand dollars you say?" Bill replied probably thinking already of how much he could buy with that money…meth and other drugs of course. He turned towards my mom who was still flailing on the floor and probably did not hear about the ten grand.

"Look at me while I am talking to you!" Francisco added with a serious voice "I'm talking serious business here, so you better listen carefully!"

"I'm listening" my father replied, "So what for?"

"My intention is to exchange this money for your daughter."

Those words hit me like a huge hammer in the back of my head and I have to admit that I did not believe it at first. I thought that it was some kind of joke or something, but soon enough I learned that Francisco was serious about it and even scarier was the fact that my father's eyes said that he was thinking about it.

I was confused and so was my father.

"So, you're gonna pay me ten grand to have sex with her?" he asked Francisco who nodded negatively.

"You did not understand my proposition, for ten thousand dollars I'll get to raise your daughter as my own; you get the money and I get Jamie, a fair trade and no further questions asked." Francisco replied and reached the inner pocket of his jacket.

I could not stay by the door anymore, and I ran and fell to my father's feet.

"Please daddy, don't do this…I'm begging you, please!" but he pushed me away with his foot.

"Stop crying like a little child, can't you see that I am doing business here?" he said to me and did not even look at me. All he could think about was that ten thousand dollars.

After a few moments of silence, Bill grins at Francisco who was standing there waiting for an answer.

"So, do we have a deal?" he broke the silence seeing that my father kept thinking about it.

"I don't believe you! Ten thousand dollars is a lot of money…you have to prove it to me that you really have the money!"

Seeing my father's reluctance, Francisco pulls out $10,000 in all hundreds and puts it on the table.

"Do you believe me now? Now the money it's on the table… it's your call!"

My father looked at the cash for a couple of moments trying to figure out if was fake or all real. That money dazzled his eyes and I could see how he was already forgetting about me…

"So let me get this straight" Bill snapped out of his trance. Now he was much more jovial and willing to have a 'decent' conversation. "You're gonna adopt Jaime like she's your own daughter or something…I don't get exactly what you mean.

"Well, kind of… but that's nothing you should be concerned about." Francisco replied, "I can assure you that she will be well taken care of, and have a much better life."

My father fell in his thoughts and during this time, my mom managed to get up from the floor and even grasp a little bit of the conversation…enough to know that there was a lot of money on the table.

"Bill…what are we going to do Bill? Ten grand, that's a lot of money you know…" she mumbled disturbing my father from his thinking.

"Don't you think I know that?" he shouted at her "And it's, what I am going to do not what we… I call the shots in this house!"

I tried to plead with my father, but he could not hear me…so I went to my mother hoping I could find a little bit of compassion in her…

"Mommy, don't let daddy sell me… I don't wanna go away; pleaseee mom…tell him I don't wanna leave!" but my mother was deaf with the reflection of the cash in her eyes.

"Hush girl…" she said to me looking at the $10,000 in hundreds that was sitting on the table.

It was clear to me that in that moment I was lost! I would on my own as my parents reactions told me that $10,000 meant more to them than their own flesh and blood.

Meanwhile, Francisco was still dealing with my father who still had a couple of issues he needed to clear up.

"Will she be able to visit us even if we take the money?" my mother interrupted. It looked like she still had a little bit of humanity in her veins, but that was not enough to take me off the table.

Francisco looked at her trying to find the best answer.

"Well, she will be under my supervision" he replied "and you see, if I consider it to be appropriate, then she could visit you, but I would not count on that; I hope you understand why I cannot give you a straight answer. Alright let's talk about the money now!"

My mother bit her lip with remorse probably, but that did not make her say stop!

"It's a lot of money for Christ's sake…" she added.

"Let's keep Christ out of our transaction ok?" Francisco quickly responded.

"I am your daughter mom…don't you love me at least a little bit, am I that insignificant to you?" I cried out with all the strength I had left, but no one heard me as they were focused on the cash.

"You are our daughter indeed, and that means we own you and can do whatever we want with you" Bill responded arrogantly. "Now shut up!"

I swallowed my words as it was useless to defend my cause anymore.

"You don't own me," I said mostly to myself but I guess that my father heard me mumbling and looked at me for a split of a second without saying anything, then his eyes fell back on the table where the money was waiting for him.

"Ahh forget it, she's all yours" and he grabbed the cash with the joy of a little kid who just received some candy.

I dropped my jaw in shock because I was still hoping to the last moment that they would decline the offer…but that only happened in my dreams and now I found myself in a situation with no escape.

Tears were rolling down my face, but no one in that room seemed to really care about me. They were more focused on the money I could make for them. Therefore, my fate was sealed in a blink of an eye where everyone was happy with their transaction except for me; I was hopeless.

Francisco pulled out some custody paper work. I will need both of you to sign by all of the X's.

"Great then, it means we have a deal!"

My father shakes his head, but Francisco wanted to make sure that both my parents agreed to what they signed off on.

"I just want to be clear…you know, because I don't want to have you turn around and discover that you have went to the police or anything because I will not stand for it. Think well about it, as your word and your signatures will seal this deal forever!" he said to my father who was in nirvana by now knowing that he had gotten his hands on $10,000.

"I told you, man, she's yours…you can take her right now!" my father replied and mom inhaled like she wanted to say something but didn't say anything. She went back into the bedroom and I could hear that she was mourning as if I was already dead…but I was still very much alive.

Now, Francisco turned towards me…

"Jamie, pack your things, we're leaving in a few moments!"

When hearing about 'my things', my father started laughing.

"She does not have any 'things' to take…just her, if you want extra stuff it's going to cost you some more dollars. I know you have money, so this is not going to be a problem for you…am I right?"

Francisco looked at Bill rather reluctantly. He hated dealing with sleazy people like him and was trying his best not to punch him right in the face.

"Alright then, a simple change of clothes will do…and then we are gone!"

"No, no no…don't put your problems in my hands." my father replied arrogantly. "From where I stand, she is your problem now, so if she needs more clothes, you'd better buy them for her…don't ask nothing of me, cause I don't really care!"

Francisco lost it at that moment…

"Okay" he looked back at me and smiled for a split second and pulled out his gun.

"You begged for this!" and he shot Bill in the leg.

Everyone except Francisco started screaming including me, but my father was the only one screaming in agony. My mother was backed against the wall in shock, she wasn't even blinking as Francisco got on the ground and pushed the barrel of the gun into my father's leg.

"Where did you say her clothes were again?" he asked my father who was squirming in pain "I did not hear you…can you talk louder… I'm a little hard of hearing kinda like you…" Francisco kept 'teasing' him but my father did not say a word.

"You're useless…" Francisco concluded and looked at me again "Go get whatever you like and let's go!"

I could not believe the scene I was witnessing and I was in shock myself. My whole body started acting weird and my ears made no exception…I could not hear properly anymore as a freaking thunder was roaring in my eardrums and my eyes kept staring at Bill's leg.

At first, I did not know how to react and I was looking kinda at the both of them at the same time… and my slowness began to annoy Francisco.

"Jaime, did you hear me? Go get your stuff, we have to leave like 15 minutes ago…go get it…now!"

Francisco's stare helped me snap out of my trance and I nodded and ran to the other room where the wardrobe was. As I was stuffing random things into a trash bag I could hear my mother in the living room.

"Why did you shoot him huh? Why? What harm has he done to you?" and she was barely breathing.

I have no idea what the look on Francisco's face was, but his voice was calmer than ever.

"You wanna know why? Well, let me tell you why. I don't know what you might be thinking, but your husband is a very stubborn man, with rather disrespectful behavior. Disrespecting me can get you killed on the streets…he's lucky I shot him in the leg and not in his head."

"See, he's still alive," he said while pushing hard on Bill's leg "he's gonna be just fine" but Bill's screams told a different story.

When I returned to the living room, I found Francisco fixing his suit and his gold locket around his neck.

"All set?" he asked and I nodded.

My father was still rolling on the floor with his leg in a blood bath and my mother was next to him trying to help him the best that she could…

She was more suffocating him than providing any kind of help.

"This business venture has truly been a pleasure to me," said Francisco as he was heading to the door "Ohh and you'd better take him to a hospital…you don't wanna have him bleeding to death in here…put that ten grand to work right away."

Even though my father was lying on the floor with his leg busted, he still thought he could make a threat.

"One day, I'll get my hands on you and you are a dead man!"

Francisco laughed in his face…

"Ohh I dare you to…I'm looking forward to that day!"

"Now, take a last look at this nightmare…this is the last time you're ever gonna see it," he said to me as he was pulling the door shut.

As I looked back, I felt bad for my parents for a split second until remembering that they had just sold me as if I were their slave or something. It's easy to understand that I had mixed feelings, and I did not even know if I should say goodbye or not. As the door was closing I could see how my mother was freaking out next to my father not knowing what to do. Thus, I kept my words to myself as they seemed oblivious to the fact that I was leaving for good.

Francisco noticed my sadness…

"Don't be sad, there was nothing good waiting for you in this house…if they were willing to sell you for 10 Gs, who knows what else they were capable of."

I was not in the mood to talk, so I just looked up at him and followed him without saying a word. What else could be said?

"Let's go home now," he said to me and grabbed my shoulder like he was my older brother.

Chapter 3

My new home

WE GOT TO THE CAR AND HE DROVE OFF TO THE OTHER side of the state. I had no idea where his house was and I really didn't care...I was numb... I laid my head against the window and looked aimlessly at the cars and the strangers walking on the streets.

When Francisco finally pulled the car up in front of his house, I refused to look at it. I felt like I was some kind of traitor, but in fact, things were much more complicated than that and judging that situation as being black or white was close to impossible.

He poked me "Hey...pick your head up, don't you wanna look at your new home?"

"What else could I do now?" I said to myself as I turned my head towards this huge house that looked rather like a palace.

The wicked smile on his face said more than a thousand words, and as he leaned towards me, I turned further away from him until I was one with the door of the car.

"I ain't gonna bite you...you know? Stop acting like I am the enemy here, cause I'm not...and so you know, I did you huge favor over there, taking you out of that hornet's nest."

I refused to give him on an answer or even acknowledge his words…and then he got really pissed off.

"Look, I know you think that I am the bad guy here…and you're not the first girl I 'bought' from junkie parents like yours. I catch a young kid like yourself pushing themselves on the streets and take them away from a bad situation and place them in a good one." He said and kinda forced me to look into his eyes. "I am not a saint and I don't do charity; that means that you will work for me, but in return, I will see to it that you receive a proper education and a beautiful place to live…something your parents would have never given to you, so you should consider yourself real lucky that I found you. And I will also teach you something else…some life lessons the school will never teach you, how to control your own destiny. Don't you think this is a fair deal?"

I tried as much as I could to avoid his eyes and when I could I gazed through the window in the opposite direction…while trying to control my tears.

"You'll be amazed of what I can teach you" he continued "I'll give you the keys to a man's heart and you'll learn how to twist and play with it until he gives you exactly what you want. Come now, let's go inside."

I wanted to go home, and that was exactly what I said to him… almost screaming…

"I want to go home nooww!"

He smiled and turned his head looking at his mansion…then pointed towards it.

"This is home now. You can't possibly call that filth hole a home and you and I both know that you did not want to spend another moment in there; now let's go, you'll like it in here, trust me."

"I can't believe you shot my father" my words exploded in a burst of anger.

"He deserved it… and I would not call him a father, someone who is willing to sell their children for whatever sum of money."

His words were indeed to the point, but still… you cannot turn blood into water overnight no matter how bad the situation.

I looked at the house crying but I could not believe how beautiful it was. The more I analyzed it the more I was amazed by it. From the exterior, it looked like it had 3 stories with huge windows and bright white walls. This was the dream house of any girl who planned to have a family with kids, a loving husband and everything that comes with it. I was no wife though and had no kids… I was just a lost little girl with no one.

He reached and wiped my tears like a loving father would do to his baby girl.

"Don't cry…you'll be safe here, trust me; now let's go!"

He opened the door of the car, but before I got out, I took another look at the house and I must say that I was astonished by it. I could have looked at it a full day and still not gotten enough. And he saw that on my face…

"Nice isn't it? It sure does look nice…and trust me…it's even better on the inside."

His words seemed genuine, so I got out of the car with him leading the way.

"You're going to be just fine, trust me and I can't wait to see Bob's face," he said to me smiling.

I have never heard him mentioning that name, so I was a little bit shocked when he did it at the last moment.

"Bob? What Bob. I didn't…" I said confused and he turned towards me and grabbed my shoulder shaking it.

"Ohh, My bad…I forgot to mention. Bob is my business partner, you see, we share this house together and each of us manages one-half of our employees. He's a good guy, don't worry…with a bad temper though, but a good guy nonetheless."

Things started to get complicated where at first it was just me and Francisco, now there was Bob and god knew who else was living in that house.

"Is that right…" I said and followed him.

"Come, I'll show you your room, I bet you'll love it!" he said and invited me to the front door, which was in itself a work of art. Exquisite wooden sculptures and glasswork that made you think that this was the door of a museum and not of a regular home.

"It opens fairly easy," he said to me and pushed it slightly.

I have no idea what mechanism it had but you could open it with the push of a finger…of course in the case where it was not locked.

When I first entered, I was amazed by the tall ceilings that were somewhere around 10 feet above my head.

My first reaction was "WOW" and I bet I looked like a cave girl who sees fire for the first time.

"Pretty impressive huh?" he smiled at me "Now let me show you to your room…that will be next to another girl that is about your age! I am sure that you will become the best of friends in no time!"

"Yeah right…" I said to myself but I did not want to let it out because I did not want to get into even more trouble. Even though I was just 13 back then, life had already taught me that sometimes it's best to keep your mouth shut if you want to get out of a bad situation in one piece.

I kept looking around as I was walking in the hallway behind Francisco. There were all kinds of fancy paintings on the walls, thus my eyes were drawn in all directions at the same time.

"We're here," he said to me waking me up from my trance.

"Here where?" I asked confused as we had stopped in front of a door.

He knocked and opened the door sticking his head through the crack.

"Heeyy" the voice of a girl could be heard.

"Wassup?" Francisco asked cordially which made me curious.

"Come…meet Tina," he said to me and pulled me inside.

Tina was reading from a thick book she was sitting on the bed… a ginormous bed I might add. A drastic difference from my mattress on the floor back home, Tina's bedroom was a dream.

"I'm glad you're reading" Francisco added and the girl jumped and hugged him leaving the book on the bed.

"It's a good book you know!" she replied and kissed him on the cheek.

I was shocked to see how fond of him this little girl was, considering the fact that she was, in fact, working for him. God works in a mysterious way indeed…if this had anything to do with Him anyway.

When she finished with Francisco and all that hugging, she turned her attention towards me and studied me for a moment.

"Let me introduce you to your new neighbor…" Francisco smiled.

"This is Tina." I forced a "hi" out of my mouth. "And this is Jamie" and then she said "hi".

There was a little bit of tension in the air…I don't know, probably she thought that I was taking him from her or something. We all know how little girls have all kinds of crushes on the wrong people. We in our situation, were little girls only on our birth certificates… we had seen things some people would pray not to experience in their lifetime.

After meeting Tina I was like "And now what?" I was expecting to receive my own room but all of a sudden a baby was heard crying.

Francisco heard it too and he got alarmed immediately.

"Opps, this is my call, if you could excuse me, ladies, I have to go now. I will leave you two to get acquainted. Tina, if you could show Jamie around, that would be great!"

"Don't worry, I will be the best guide ever" Tina smiled and Francisco disappeared from the room.

"Ohh and you'll meet Bob tomorrow morning most likely!" Francisco shouted as he was running in the hallway.

"Ok ok" I replied and returned to my awkwardness. I was not the sociable type who would get along with anyone at any time. It took time for me to open up and trust people, no doubt because of the countless traumas I had experienced.

Tina, on the other hand, was rather the opposite, she smiled a lot and was outgoing. I kept wondering if she went through this transformation after Francisco had found her or if she had been like that from birth. It's kinda hard to be traumatized and happy at the same time…thus you can see why I was a bit puzzled by this young girl.

I started looking around the room and all the stuff that it was packed with. Starting with the bed, a leather couch, nice chairs, a huge mirror any girl would love and a wardrobe filled with expensive clothes. The view was also amazing as it allowed us to see into a beautifully arranged garden with fresh cut grass and all kinds of flowers and trees.

"Not bad huh?" she said to me as I kept looking around in awe.

"Aha" I mumbled but I would have traded material wealth for true parental love any day. I did not have such luck, unfortunately.

"And this is not all you know… this whole house it's like a labyrinth filled with all kinds of cool stuff…you'll see" she added and I just could not help it and started crying suddenly.

Tina quickly embraced me as I was about to fall on my knees.

"It's okay…you're okay, please don't cry…it's not worth it trust me, you're wasting your tears and energy in vain!"

"I wish I could…but it's hard. You don't understand, my parents sold me like I meant nothing to them. They gave me away, just like that, for 10 thousand dollars…to someone, they did not even know. I could be dead right now for God's sakes and they could care less about that. I just can't believe they would do such a thing to their own daughter. They are both monsters!" I replied but Tina disapproved.

"Hmm, I would not call them monsters…" she said but I did not agree with her.

"You don't know them…they are horrible!" I ground my teeth and pushed away from her with my back against the wall covering my eyes with my hands.

"I know exactly how you are feeling, trust me." Tina said to me and sat next to me with her back against the wall. "I was just brought here a few weeks ago and like you, I was sold by my father for money…"

"You too?" I asked baffled "Is there anyone else here like us?"

"Not that I know of…" she said but that was a different conversation.

"And you're ok with that? I see you're smiling and…"

"Ehh…" she replied and made that "whatever" sign with her hand in the air. "Who would be ok with being sold just like a slave? The thing is…I realized after the first night when I cried continuously that it's not worth it, you know. And over the next week, my mind started to change as I thought more and more about it. The 'evil' is done and we can change things now…and as for my father and your father now…if they sold us like we were cattle to them, it means that they did not deserve us in the first place…am I right? Forget them, they don't deserve us!"

I looked at her and nodded…she was kinda right after all. I was in a bad situation and I was crying for the people who had put me in it in the first place…how crazy is that.

"God has a path and a plan for all of us…you should always keep that in mind!" she added and I almost laughed.

"God? What does God have to do with what is happening to us…I don't wanna be disrespectful but no real God would let this happen to us. This is how I see things…God is supposed to love us, this doesn't feel like love" I replied and she nodded negatively.

"You have so much to learn…" then Tina replied and reached for her book.

I was tired and not much in a mood for conversation. I had gone through enough already and wanted to get some rest.

"Can you please take me to my room?" I said to Tina who was shuffling aimlessly through the pages of her book. "I just want to go to sleep…we can talk later."

"Sure thing" she smiled at me and put her book down again. "Follow me."

We exited her room and walked a few steps on the same hallway until we reached another door.

"This is it…I'm sure you're gonna like it a lot!" she added as I looked around the room. It was as nice as hers.

"It's ok" I replied and she smiled at me.

"It's better than ok, trust me…and if you do what they tell you and provide for them, then we're all gonna be happy!"

"We clearly have different definitions of happiness," I thought to myself as I went to test the bed.

"I have to go now, but you let me know if you need anything else ok?" she said and left the room.

"I will…" I mumbled and tried to stretch a smile.

"Good night then…see you later!"

After she closed the door, I left my bag on the floor and started 'unpacking' the little things I managed to take from my parents' house. As I was unpacking my things and carefully arranging them in the drawers, I could not help rewinding in my head the events that had just happened earlier that night. I kept asking how I had gotten myself into this mess. I tried to understand if I had any blame in it, but the more I thought about it, the more the devastation of the situation hit me.

"I just wanna die!" I mumbled and walked in front of the huge mirror that was stuck to one of the walls in my room.

My face was traumatized and there were layers over layers of tears that had dried up on my cheeks. I kept grinding my teeth with anger, but I guess it was rather despair and a feeling of abandonment. I felt like my body and my soul did not belong to me anymore and I was just a mere shadow of the girl I used to be before.

Tears kept falling down as I stood there in front of the mirror. I wanted to stop crying but I just could not do it…I was not in control anymore.

"Whyyyy???!" I screamed suddenly and hit the bottom of the mirror with my right foot.

A piece of it broke off falling on the floor.

"Oh God, what have I done?" I said scared and tried to put it back;

I struggled for a few moments until I realized that I could not do anything about it…but then this crazy thought came to my mind.

"I should end it right here, right now!" I said to myself and grabbed the shard of glass. I pushed it against my neck while still looking into the mirror. "I don't care…Francisco could as well go and get his money back from my parents…it's not my problem!"

I could feel as the glass began to cut through the outer cells of my skin and I wished I could continue to the end…but again something would not let me take my own life, at least not at that moment.

"Noo" I cried out "Why God, why can't I do it? I'm sick of this life!"

I ran and threw myself on the bed. I could not stand looking at my image in the mirror…as there was nothing for me to see. After carefully hiding that piece of glass for safe keeping under the mattress, I turned around with my face toward the ceiling and kept looking up… I tried to think of a way out, but there was none. Wherever I looked, all I could see were dead ends and helpless situations.

Eventually, my eyes closed and I fell asleep. I cannot tell exactly when that happened or how much I cried after I laid in bed.

When I woke up in the morning, I had this terrible headache and my body was hurting as if Bill had beaten me for 5 straight hours the previous night. I was not in the mood for anything and all I wanted was not to be disturbed by anyone…but this was not home and there were rules I had to follow regardless of whether I liked them or not.

Around 8 a.m., we were supposed to have breakfast, and this meant we all gathered in the kitchen. Tina was already there drinking orange juice when I got there. She waved at me with her usual smile.

"Did you sleep okay?" she asked me while sipping from her glass.

"It was fine" I replied with all the enthusiasm I could muster at the time. I was lying nonetheless.

"The first night is always the hardest, but you'll get used to it in no time…trust me; I am talking from experience!" she mumbled but I was really not in the mood for conversation.

"Ehh, we'll see."

"Cheer up girl, we're gonna be fine!" she put her glass on the table and hugged me, shaking me a few times.

"You're crazy" was my reply and she gladly agreed with me.

"Yeah, I know…I have to tell you something okay?"

I nodded yes, so she took a deep breath and started talking faster and faster but with a lot of emotion in her voice.

"You see," she said looking straight into my eyes as much as I tried to avoid her look. "I cannot really remember the last time when I had my own bed. My dad used to sell everything he could get his hands on just to buy drugs, so our home was an empty space with no furniture. Just garbage all over the place and used needles. The closest notion of a bed I had was just a pile of cardboards stacked one on top of another… and now I have this…"

I felt really sorry for her, and her words made me understand that some people had it even harder than me.

"I am sorry to hear this" I replied, but I could never find the right words to help Tina feel better.

"Don't worry" she smiled at me, but tears were falling down her face this time as she was visibly affected by the things she had been forced to go through. "That's all in the past now…it can't hurt us anymore, right?"

I did not know what to say about the hurting part, but it was clear to me that no child should go through such terrible things.

We did not get to discuss anything else because Francisco walked in along with Bob. Bob was this well-built man around 6 feet 3 inches with a pair of 'mean eyes' as I used to call them at first. He looked like he could see through you…the kind of man you could never lie to regardless of how much of an actor you thought yourself to be.

"Hi girls" both Francisco and Bob saluted us and then Francisco put two plates filled with food on the table.

I quickly grabbed the fork and started digging in. I was starving and could not remember when the last time I had a decent meal was.

"Jaime, this is Bob…Bob…Jamie."

I rolled my eyes and looked at him without moving my head. I was too busy eating, but I still said a short 'Hi' in between bites.

Tina was busy eating too; Francisco grabbed a chair and sat close to me at the table, while Bob was still standing.

"I trust we had a good first night?" he said and poured a glass of juice sipping a few times.

"Aha" I replied with my mouth full.

"Great then…this is great news Jamie!" he replied smiling "Now, let me introduce you properly! This is Bob, my business partner so to speak, and you, my dear, will be under his direct care and supervision! Trust me, you could not be in better hands!" he clapped his hands while Bob was smiling cunningly from two feet away.

"Hurry up and finish that." Bob intervened "We have a lot on our plate today, so we need to move fast!" He had a rather squeaky voice for a man his size. I mean, I was waiting to hear one of those classic gorilla voices, and that's why I was a little bit surprised to hear him speak. Francisco turned his head slowly and from the look on his face, it was clear that he knew nothing about that 'rush'.

"And what's with all the hurrying up?" he asked looking straight at Bob.

"You know man" Bob quickly defended himself "I need to show her the ropes, the ins and outs… she's fresh so I need to brief her a little bit about this business; there's things she needs to know."

"Alright then" Francisco replied with a calmed voice "But keep in mind that this is not a late night; I want them up for service tomorrow morning; don't forget that!"

"That is why I want to get them up and running asap and I'll be taking Tina out too!"

She stopped eating all of a sudden when she heard that she had to go out too… she kept looking at Bob confused because she knew nothing about his plans for her.

"Is there a reason behind your need for Tina?" Francisco insisted.

"Yeah, big money…if this gig gets on, we'll make a great deal of cash." Bob replied but Francisco was still unconvinced by it.

"Do you know these people? I mean, have you checked them out to make sure everything will be ok?"

"Of course partner, you know me, I always do!" Bob added and Francisco smiled satisfied.

"You know they are not like the rest…that's all I'm sayin'" he said and then turned his head towards us.

"Girls, it looks like you're both going on a little field trip together. This is going to work perfectly; Tina, you can teach Jamie a thing or two along the way alright?"

Tina nodded and smiled at him "Of course Francisco, don't you worry, I'll be the best teacher ever!"

"We're good then…and I'll see you both for service in the morning okay?"

We both nodded, but I had no idea what that 'service' meant. I mean, I suspected something but I did not have the courage to ask about it.

"I guess, I'm going to find out when the time comes" I thought to myself and tried to finish the food on my plate. I was still hungry, but I was too embarrassed to ask for more…that breakfast was better than the slop I used to have back at my parent's place…

Francisco left the kitchen soon after with a wide smile on his face.

After Francisco left the kitchen, Bob took his chair and simply looked at how we were eating…probably timing us with his eyes.

We soon learned that he was doing just that. When I was about to take my last bite, he grabbed the plates from the table and took them to the trash. Tina still had a lot on her plate, but Bob did not really care about that aspect. He focused only on what he had to do!

"Alright" he said after he turned around "I think you've had enough for the time being…you'll have more later, but right now we need to go as we have a schedule to stick to…so get dressed asap! The clock is ticking…tic toc…tic toc!"

Bob went to the window to smoke a cigarette, and during this time, both Tina and me were supposed to get ready. I was dying of curiosity though, so I had to ask!

"Where are we going now Tina?…I don't understand!" I asked her and she went in a thoughtful mood.

"Hmm…how did Francisco put it? We're not window display products…that's right, we're kinda exclusive for exclusive people!"

Her words struck me like a bullet and I was afraid to think that I was right about what was going through my mind at that moment.

"And that would be what exactly?!" I insisted trying to appear completely oblivious.

"Hmm…" she hummed for a few seconds. "Well Jamie, basically we'll be the kind of working girls that never go out in the streets. We'll rather have sex only after private appointments are made, away from people's eyes and more importantly away from the cops…they can really be a pain."

"I am scared." I replied with a trembling voice "What if they just don't want us to run…I mean, if no one knows about us, it's easier for them to control us!"

"That's an idea…but anyway, it's better that way for everybody… you've seen what's out there right?"

I nodded slightly trying to delete those scenes from my memory. A few moments of complete silence followed where both of us thought of what to say next. Bob was still by the window puffing nervously; he would shed an eye towards us every once in a while but did not say a word.

"I wanna ask you something…If I…" Tina broke the silence eventually.

"Yeah, sure…what is it?"

"When was your first time? I don't wanna sound like…"

"It's ok, don't worry" I interrupted her "I don't mind" and threw her a smile. "It happened a few weeks ago and it was a complete disaster, I bled everywhere…and the pain…oh my God, was terrible!"

"Well the first time it's always the messiest…as for the pain, it will go away eventually, you'll see!" She replied and grabbed my hand.

"I hope you're right" I stuttered, then thought about it again, "anyway, even if it hurts, I'm fine with it…that way I will never forget."

Bob kept looking at us more and more insistently, and this was the signal for us that we had to gear up. His smoke was almost done.

"I think it's time" Tina giggled at me and rushed to her room. "We'd better get ready before Bob loses it…"

Her words calmed me more than her smiling face ever could, so as a result I ran to my room and started looking for something I could wear. I had no idea where I was going so a pair of tights and a shirt would do. I did not own any make up back home and the previous night when I left, I did not get to take anything from my mother's drawers.

For that reason, I came out way sooner than Tina who was prepping herself quite carefully. I knocked at the door, and entered before she could say 'come in' and I was astonished by what I saw.

She was wearing this gorgeous red dress with white ornaments with her hair falling freely on her half exposed back. Tina was looking like a princess, but that did not matter at all…at least not to Bob and Francisco who only cared about the money.

"Wow girl…you look…" I tried to say but she did not let me finish.

"Fancy right?" she smiled and took another look in the mirror. "Every time I wear this dress, my clients are baffled and I even get tips. Which is pretty nice!"

"Yeah, kinda…" I replied not wanting to ruin her mood.

It was a shame though that we had to wear such nice dresses for such hideous reasons.

"I'm ready…" she added "We should go now…waiting is the last thing Bob likes to do…and you don't wanna see him mad, trust me!" she giggled and went out right in front of Bob who was probably coming to take us out by the ears.

"Tina…you look nice!" he complimented her and she made a pirouette right there in the hallway. Two seconds later, he focused his attention on me and analyzed my outfit…and I could see it in his eyes that he was not pleased.

"You look good too," he said to me "but there are improvements you could make!"

"I did not have that many clothes…so…" I tried to defend myself and he looked like he understood.

"Yeah, yeah…this is your first day anyway, so let it be…but from now on, I wanna see both of you looking like the bell of the ball! Understood? The finer you look, the more money I make…and that makes me happy! You don't wanna make me sad…" he said and pointed his index towards me mostly.

I felt guilty somehow, but I didn't know how to put a proper outfit together. It wasn't like I had a lot of practice.

"I understand…" I replied and put my head down. I was aware that there was no room for debate there.

Chapter 4

First day on the job

W E GOT INTO THE CAR, AND BOB STARTED DRIVING towards a destination only he knew. Before he even drove half a mile he threw something in the back seat where we were sitting.

"I hope none of you are on your periods?!" he said and turned his head towards us.

We both shook our heads telling him that we were not.

"Good then...good! You should start taking those pills like right now. We don't have time to lose." He added, but I had no idea what those were so I felt the need to ask.

"What are these things?"

"Birth control baby girl... you don't need no kids right now. Kids are bad for business... and these fellows we're dealing with really don't like wearing any protection...I mean, who does? I know I prefer not to...if you know what I mean..." he replied with a wicked smile on his face; I was disgusted.

I grabbed one packet...as he had thrown a bunch of them, 4 or 5 I guess. As I pulled one of the tablets out, I kept looking at Tina to see if she was going to take them. She did not seem to have any issues, so I lifted my shoulders trying to let her know I had no idea what to do.

She nodded yes…then I thought, "What else could I do?" and I popped one out and into my mouth…I had no other alternative.

That was my first time in life taking birth control pills…only God knew what else would follow.

As I snapped out of my own drama, I could see where Bob had taken us. A rough area that looked like a war had been fought there just a few weeks before; hookers left and right wherever you looked. They clearly knew who Bob was, but I wasn't sure which ones had him as a pimp.

I was new to this world still, and I did not know too much about how things worked or what the general rules were.

All of a sudden I saw this older hooker getting closer to the car and Bob rolled down the window. She was so excited you'd think she had seen the Pope himself or something, she bent down and kissed Bob on both his cheeks.

"Wassup baby" she says to him smiling.

"Don't baby me now…I'm not in the mood for it…tell me, you got it?"

"Right here…the girls hit it real big last night…I hope you're pleased." And she handed him a bag with cash.

Bob looked at the bag for a few brief moments and put it in the glove compartment.

"I would be pleased if you would hit it big every day…We have the absolute best, you should keep that in mind!" he replied and caused the hooker to blush a little bit.

"Ohh Bob, your too much…" she replied, and Bob prepared to leave.

As he was rolling up the window, she remembered something.

"Ugh…we had a little hiccup though…" she added and quickly caught Bob's interest.

"Say what?" he said arching his eyebrows.

"Suzy kinda had a rough night with this guy… and she…"

"Can she work?" Bob insisted and I could see how he was slowly losing his temper.

"Well, she's in really bad shape right now…I don't know what to say!" she mumbled with a worried look on her face.

Bob facial expression changed.

"She was beaten pretty badly..." the hooker added.

"What...who is this trick?" Bob asked clearly agitated at this point.

"You must know him...Alejandro...he's a frequent at the bar, Mexican guy, large moustache; you can't miss him."

"Okay, I'll handle this!"

"Fine baby, see you tomorrow!" she smiled at him, and looked at us in the back for a couple of moments with a bit of sadness in her eyes and walked away.

The next second Bob drove away, but I followed her with my eyes for a couple of moments and I saw how she went back to the other girls and they chatted for a couple of moments.

After taking a turn, I could not see them anymore, but that was not an issue because we were still going to have action...of another kind this time. It did not take more than 2 or 3 minutes and we reached the bar the hooker was talking about. Bob was bursting with anger, I could see it on his face; the veins of his temple were about to pop.

I was scared, and kept my mouth shut because I suspected that something very serious was about to happen. He reached in the glove compartment and grabbed a pair of black gloves; he quickly put them on and opened the door of the car.

"You two, stay in the car and wait; I'll be back in a couple of minutes" he said as he was about to shut the door closed.

That was when I opened my mouth for some reason...I quickly regretted it, but it was too late.

"Are you at least going to ask him if he did anything in the first place?" I asked Bob and he looked at me with a question mark on his face. Tina was also shocked because I dared to challenge Bob's authority and judgment.

"What...? Why would she lie to me?" he replied with an irritated voice.

"Maybe she wanted revenge on him? Maybe there has been something between them and now she just wants him hurt... there could be a hundred reasons if you think about it!"

"You're the thinking type huh?" he mumbled and grins at me. "If that's the case, why don't you come with me right now and I'll show you what a liar looks like alright? Get out of the car and follow me!"

Tina looked angrily at me. It was clear that she was blaming me already for opening my mouth…she did not say a word though.

Bob opened the back door for us and we got out of the car. The second we entered through the door of that bar, Bob started scanning the place trying to spot the guy. After a few moments, Bob sees him at the bar sitting on one of those tall chairs sipping on a glass of jack.

"Stay close to me and don't say a word!" he said and started walking towards Alejandro.

The guy was oblivious to our presence and minding his own business. Bob stops three inches behind him.

"Excuse me." said Bob but Alejandro did not acknowledge him.

"Get lost, I'm busy!" he finally said without even looking.

"Are you Alejandro?" Bob insisted.

"Man are you suicidal? I said get lost? Which part didn't you understand?" he replied turning around at the same time.

"Oh my bad" he exclaimed and his eyes widened when realizing that he was talking to Bob. "Man, I did not know it was you, sorry about that…I just…"

"Do you have any idea why I am here?" Bob interrupted him.

Alejandro lifted his shoulders… playing the innocent card.

"The slightest idea?" Bob asked again.

"I swear I gave her exactly what she asked for…so I don't get why you're so pissed off right now!" Alejandro mumbled looking around trying to see if anyone was going come to his defense. Unfortunately it was not his lucky day as everyone knew who Bob was and they only stopped to witness the event. Nobody dared to get involved.

"It looks like my girl is in a pretty bad shape right now and all because of you… you must have felt like a real tough guy when you were hitting a defenseless woman huh?" Bob replied and acted like he was about to hit Alejandro who was ready to dodge the blow.

"I swear I did not lay a finger on her man; she's lying…I'm telling you, I don't know why she said those things but I did not touch her."

Alejandro defended himself, but Bob did not look like he was believing a single word.

"Hmm, I don't know why, but I find it hard to trust crooks like yourself...you've got something on your face that makes me not trust you!" Bob added and Alejandro started touching his face probably trying to feel if there was something stuck to it.

"I'm innocent man...I don't know why she's saying those things...you know me, I never touched any of your girls!"

"All I know" Bob replied nervously "Is that one of my girls is wasted and when her body and face look bad...she cannot make money for me! And I can't let 'tough' guys like you mess with my profits!"

Bob's voice raised in pitch and I could tell that he was about to do something. I was scared so I took one step back...and he felt that.

"Don't move, I said!" he turned his head and yelled at me; my body froze in that moment.

That half a second was all Alejandro needed, so he grabbed a beer bottle from the bar and slammed Bob over the head with it. The bottle broke into a hundred pieces and beer was splashed all over the place...my shirt was soaking in it...and you'd think that this was Bob's end...but that was far from it.

Alejandro ran away the moment he hit Bob with that bottle, but he did not get too far because Bob grabbed his gun and started shooting aimlessly in Alejandro's direction.

Eventually, one bullet hit Alejandro in the leg and he stumbled over the tables falling on the floor eventually.

Bob looked at me angrily...

"What did I tell you? "Don't move!" and he raised his backhand ready to slap me. I winched and prepared for the hit...my eyes were closed. His hand never touched me as he stopped midway through... he shook his head.

"You're lucky you have an appointment today...otherwise..."

He quickly moved his focus towards Alejandro who was bleeding and screaming on the floor. Bob walked slowly towards him and grabbed him by the back of his head...

"How did you think this would play out?" he said with a weird satisfaction in his voice then hit the man with the back of his gun in the ribs. Alejandro weeps…

"Forgive me man…" Alejandro begged but Bob was not into any of that.

"I ain't Mother Mary to spread forgiveness all around me fool… you messed up my girl and that will cost me a couple of thousand dollars…who's gonna give me that money huh? You…?" Bob replied and slapped him again.

"I'll give you the money…tell me how much and I will get you the money!"

"Just pay what you owe nothing more nothing less…2 grand by the end of the week…otherwise, I'll come looking for you again and this time I won't aim for your leg…if you know what I mean…" Bob added and slammed Alejandro's head against the floor.

"I'll give you two grand by the end of the week, I promise…" Alejandro cried out in pain.

"You'd better…" Bob mumbled and whacks him over the head with the butt of the gun. Alejandro was knocked out.

I was shocked by the sequence of events that unfolded and I kept thinking of Bob's brutality. This man was ruthless, a psychopath who did not hesitate for a second to take one's life if he messed with his money.

All of a sudden, I felt how Tina was dragging me out of the bar.

"Come on…we need to get out of here, stop staring like that" she yelled at me, but I was still lost.

Bob walked out of there victorious, and he did not seem to care that quite a lot of people saw what he did to Alejandro and that cops might find out about this incident.

"Let's go" Bob shouted at us. It was clear we had to get in the car and get out of there asap.

Bob drove us straight home from there…in perfect silence. Only the sound of the tires rubbing on the asphalt could be heard as he did not turn on the radio anymore. Tina minded her own business there in the back seat and kept gazing at the screen of her phone. I could feel that she was mad at me for causing all that mess with my 'movement'.

I took it as that and kept my mouth shut.

When we finally got home, Bob pulled the car in front of the house quite violently.

"Your clothes are ruined so get out and get ready! In one hour we need to be at the club, important people are waiting for us…upstairs you'll find all the clothes you need, so go get yourself something nice… Tina, show her how it's done!"

"Come on…" she whispered and I followed her inside the house and then upstairs.

There was this room that had been transformed into a huge closet…it looked like a shop where you could find all kinds of clothes from pants, tights to fancy dresses…you name it. Tina noticed my amazement and felt the need to provide me with an explanation.

"Some like role playing… they pay good money so Bob buys us everything we need!" she said smiling and started searching through the clothes.

"We'll need two sexy skirts tonight and two tiny tank tops," she added while shuffling through. "You ever been to a club before?"

I nodded no…

"Ohh noo…you're a club virgin huh…this is gonna be epic, trust me…I just love clubbing…" she said and pulled one tiny skirt out of the wardrobe. "This is it! Try it."

I grabbed the skirt but I could not stop wondering…

"Why do you like it so much…you go there to have sex for money!" I said to her and she started shaking her head.

"No no darling…clubbing is much more than that…you have sex indeed but you have fun too…these clients are stylish men, not like that scumbag you saw at the bar. They pay you indeed to have sex with them, but they know how to treat a woman…you will see soon enough what I am talking about!" she replied and chose a skirt for herself too.

"Here, try this top…" she said and threw me a top even smaller than the skirt. "It will look good on you, trust me!"

"If you say so…" I replied and tried them on.

When I looked in the mirror, I could tell that Tina had good taste, but I was still looking like a lady of the night nonetheless. I spinned a couple of times to take a better look from all sides.

"Oh my god, you look fabulous!" Tina exclaimed "And those hips girl…you're gonna drive those gentlemen wild! That's for sure."

"Thanks…I guess" I replied and I looked again at 'those hips'. They still looked like the hips of a 13-year-old girl who was not supposed to be in that situation.

Right as we got dressed, I heard a knock on the door. Bob was losing his patience by now.

"You ready or what?" he said through the cracked door.

"We're coming…we're coming" Tina replied joyfully and rushed to the door to close it. "You know it's not nice to spy on a girl while she is making herself pretty." She said to Bob who backed down.

"Yeah right" he mumbled, "Don't forget that we're on a tight schedule…so you'd better get moving."

In the next five minutes we were up and running and it did not take more the 15 minutes for Bob to get us to the club. He drove fast, but I guess he meant it when he said we were on a tight schedule.

The moment we reached the club I saw that we already had a table and a couch reserved. We took a seat and we were brought some drinks immediately. I realized soon that the club owners knew Bob pretty well and this was their routine so to speak. I was not fond of alcohol, but I decided to drink some…otherwise I could not get through this ordeal.

Bob took another look at me and Tina before he left to talk to someone.

"You look nice…well done Tina…now, I am sure I don't have to tell you what you gotta do in there! All I wanna know is that the client comes out satisfied and eager to see you again, alright? Now chill for a moment, I have some business to take care of." he said and went somewhere else in the club.

I could see how people were shaking his hand smiling. Bob was well known in the business and everyone who needed some fresh meat, knew he could provide it for them.

Taking advantage of his absence, I filled up my glass and started drinking the liquor...dry. Tina looked at me at first, then she realized that I was up to something, so she grabbed my glass.

"Yo..yo...what do you think you're doing?" she said alarmed.

"I will never be able to do it if I am sober...trust me, it's better if I am numb; this way I can pretend it's not even happening." I replied but she knew something else.

"Bob will kill us if we get drunk before the client comes...trust me, I know better! So, leave the glass on the table and get your act together...it's not play time anymore, you'd better get that stuck in that pretty head of yours."

In that moment I felt like prisoner, and that's exactly what I was...

"You saw what he's capable of, right? You don't want a bullet in your head tonight!" Tina insisted and I put the glass down.

"Whatever..." I replied and plunged into that leather sofa with my arms crossed.

"And another thing...you should put that smile back on your face... nobody likes to pay for an angry face!"

Tina was starting to annoy me by now, and I wanted to tell her so...I did not get the chance though because Bob came back.

"You ready ladies" he said with a smiling face.

We both nodded yes...actually Tina more than me, but I could not tell him that I did not want to do this, because I knew what would follow.

"Perfect then, let's get up...the party is about to start!" he added and made a sign that we should follow him.

Tina went first and then I followed. We when upstairs to a VIP room in the club, Bob opened the door for us smiling.

Inside, there was huge black leather sofa, a small table and a couple of three legged chairs. The walls were painted with all kinds of obscene images...twisted art. This looked exactly like the type of room where ungodly things took place on a daily basis.

"Now girls, you be good, the guest is about to get here." said Bob and right as he finished speaking there was a knock on the door.

Knock, knock, knock.

"Oh, he's here already…remember what I told you." he whispered to us and opened the door.

"Girls, this is Mayor Simon…Mayor…the girls!" Bob quickly made the introductions and I could not believe my eyes. In front of us was the actual Mayor of the city. A supposedly respectable man in his mid-fifties…a man who apparently liked to pay to have sex with little girls.

"So, how old are you girls?" he asked with the voice of Don Juan. "You look pretty young to me."

"We are old enough sir." replied Tina with a bold voice.

After a half an hour the whole ordeal was over, and the mayor left. He did not even look at us or say anything. He got dressed and exited through the back door.

Right after Mayor Simon left the room, Bob came in applauding.

"Bravo!" he exclaimed "Now get dressed, we gotta go!"

The whole dressing thing and the ride home happened in pure silence. I was not really in a mood to say anything after what had happened to me and Tina acted in solidarity.

As soon as I got back home, I went straight to my room and did not come out until morning. I did not need food or anything else, I just wanted to be alone with my thoughts.

The next day, Francisco made us go to church. I had no idea that pimps went to church…and this caused me to laugh a little with all the pain that I was feeling. He probably wanted to appease God for his many sins…who knows.

"You did a great job last night…I am very proud of you!" he whispered to us as we were sitting there. I nodded and minded my own business, which meant keeping my head down and not say a word. Life was starting to take all kinds of twisted turns for me and I was wondering what would follow next.

Chapter 5

Five years later - time for change

FIVE YEARS HAD PASSED AND SOMEHOW A NUMBNESS
had grown inside of me; I learned to become oblivious to everything.
I suppose this is the survival instinct that pushes us to do all kinds of
crazy things in order to stay alive.

Now I was sitting in my room, focused on my laptop. Tina came
in with her usual smile on her face.

"What's cookin' doc?" she laughed at me but I did not reply with
the same enthusiasm.

"Not much." I said.

"So where are you headed tonight? Any idea?" she added but I had
no answer for her.

"I don't really know…"

"Come on, it's Friday…you know Mayor Simon always books you
for Friday night…or have you forgotten that?"

"Ehh…he can miss me for a week, he'll live even if he doesn't see
me!" I replied acidly and this caused Tina to have a scared reaction.

"Girl, you're playing with fire, I'm telling you. If Bob finds out
about this…especially if it's the Mayor…you know he won't be pleased
at all!" she said with utter concern.

"C'mon…like I don't know what's gonna happen!" I said to her with a straight face "He's hit me before and he'll do it again no matter what. You'd be lying if you said you were afraid of that buffoon any longer…let's be serious!"

Tina kinda refused to answer but I was looking straight into her eyes with my eyebrows raised.

"Yeah, I'm not…but I don't like getting hit either…so…"

"Forget him!" I added and returned to my typing.

She peeked at the screen for a second and saw that I was talking to Tim.

"Don't tell me that you are talking with Tim again." she erupted.

"Okkkk but that's exactly what I am doing right now…wanna see?" I laughed.

"No thanks…" she turned her face away "I don't care, but you should stop doing that…you know that he's bad news with his motorcycle gang and everything."

"Ohh, like the guys we are forced to sleep with every night are angels or something…give me a break" I reacted and she was kinda hurt by my attitude.

"I just want you to be careful…that's all! In the end, it's your business…"

I grabbed her hand and pulled her closer.

"You have no reason to worry friend! Tim is harmless, trust me I know better!" I said to her but she still looked like she did not believe me.

"Oh God, I'm sorry for being such a brat…I've just been under a lot of stress today. I don't know why, but I have not been myself." I said to her while she was still looking at me with reluctance.

"Come, take a seat, I wanna tell you something important." I added and her eyes widened suddenly.

She came and sat.

"What is it? What happened?" she asked curiously and I could not find my words to express my intentions.

"I'm gonna tell you something, but you must promise to keep it a secret alright?"

"You are scaring me already" she replied looking at me oddly "What is it?"

"Ok…" I gasped "Tim has been helping me locate my parents and now he finally found them!"

"Whaaat?!" she exclaimed "Are you out of your mind?"

"Shh…calm down, it's not like I have killed someone! As I said, he helped me find them and I'm going to see them tonight!" I replied and she grabbed my hands.

"This is something you can't do…really, you'll put your life in serious danger!" she said to me and almost started crying. "Please don't go!"

"I understand, but I have to go…I have to face them and tell them to their face how much they have hurt me!" I replied almost coming to tears myself.

"You don't understand" she said "You don't exist to them, from the moment they sold you… let them rot in peace, this is not worth it!"

"I know…but…this is something I just have to do. I know you don't understand this but I have to go there and face them so that I can move on. I just can't go on like this, something has gotta change!"

"What makes you think they care about you…after all, they sold you for money…what better proof do you need to understand that they're just two soulless creatures?" she made her point but I still had to go.

"I am aware of all that, but the bottom line is that I have to go!"

"Fine, as you wish…but what about Mayor Simon? What are you going to do about him?" she asked, but to me, the mayor was my last concern that night.

"Hmm…the mayor…well, he can satisfy himself for the night and not spend the taxpayers money for a change" I laughed but she shook her head in disapproval.

"You're playing with fire…" she mumbled.

"I'm doing that every day baby…we're both doing it…now I have to leave, see you later." I concluded and left the room. I was supposed to meet with Tim in just a few minutes.

Before I left the house, I made sure that no one saw me. Bob was supposed to take me to the club and if he saw me going out alone he would surely stop me in my tracks. So, after I snuck out like a silent cat, I rushed to the street corner where Tim had agreed to meet me.

When I got to there, there was no sign of Tim and this worried me a little bit. The closer I was to our house the greater were the chances of Bob finding me. My heart was racing and I could feel anxiety slowly building up in every cell; I started biting my fingernails, I used to do this every time I felt stressed and overwhelmed when I was young… and this time was no different.

Eventually, I could hear the sound of the motorcycle in the distance and this helped my heart slow down a little. The moment he arrived, he pulled me onto the motorcycle with one hand. I can say with my hand on my heart that Tim is the definition of a strong man…not just physically speaking because he was the kindest man I had ever met in my life. His hard exterior did not portray for a second his warm heart.

"Phew, I thought you'd never come!" I said to him as I was holding him tight.

"You know I would never leave you hanging… right?" he replied,

"Yeah…I just…" I tried to say but he interrupted me.

"It's gonna be ok, don't worry! Hold on now…we're getting out of here!"

"You sure it's them?" I asked right before leaving.

"Positive!" he replied shortly.

"Let's go then…" I said and he drive off.

After driving for about 2 hours through the city streets, we reached a place that looked more like dumpster than a place where people would actually choose to live.

"You sure it's here?" I asked Tim disgusted by the things that I was seeing. Junkies all over the place, garbage as far as the eye could see and broken windows at almost every apartment.

"I told you I have found them, now follow me."

I followed Tim inside one of those apartment buildings, on the second floor where I witnessed a picture even more desolate than outside. I felt sorry for the people who had to live there for whatever reason. After reaching the middle of the hallway, Tim stopped and pointed at an ugly door which had almost no paint on it.

"This is it!" he said.

"Are you sure?" I asked surprised by the fact that this place looked even worse than the one I used to live in before they sold me to Francisco.

"100 percent."

"Fine then" I mumbled and prepared myself for this face to face confrontation.

"I'll be here if you need me ok? Don't be nervous, I've got your back." Tim whispered and stepped out of the way, a few feet to the side.

"I'm ok, don't worry, it will be quick!" I said and made my fist to knock.

At first I hesitated, but then I looked at Tim again and saw him making signs that I should be brave. With his support I mustered up the guts to knock. I knocked three times and hoped for an answer, but at first, nothing could be heard; it was as if the apartment had been deserted.

I put my ear to the door trying to hear something, and Tim came closer to me.

"Maybe they're not..." he tried to say but I heard something.

"Shh...quiet" I whispered to him and focused on the noises coming from the other side of the door.

There was something going on inside no doubt, and it looked like people were shuffling. This was it, where I would confront my parents for the first and last time...so, without further ado I grabbed the knob of the door and made my way inside.

The front door leads directly to the living room...it was a mess obviously, clothes and garbage all over the place, but there was no one there. I looked around trying to see if I could find anyone, and my hopes were not in vain because my father emerged from the bedroom looking at me like a total stranger. His face was all swollen and bruised. It was clear that he had been in a fight of some sort...and ended up on the wrong end of it.

"Who the heck are you?" he asked. I did not say a word and just looked at him. I felt pity and anger at the same time, but I was also disgusted by what I was witnessing.

"Are you here to drop off?" he asked again…and this time I cared to reply.

"Nope!"

"Are you a cop or something?" he insisted.

"Neither…" I said and this really pissed him off.

"Fine…then get out, I don't have time for silly games." He replied and turned around heading back toward the bedroom.

My lip was quivering, and I just felt a strange urge…I simply wanted to strangle the life out of him.

"Are you that slow that you can't remember anything?" I said and he looked at me again but with the same straight face; he didn't have a clue! The face of his only child meant nothing to him.

"You don't remember anything huh?" I burst in rage "That pathetic brain of yours is all smoked out!"

"Should I remember something that I don't?" he laughed ironically.

"You're lucky…" I took a deep breath as he turns his head.

"How's that?"

"Lucky I don't slap the crap out of you!" I added and caught his attention at the same time.

"It's Jaime," I said trying not to burst in tears.

At first, he did not believe me, and drew closer to take another look. He soon realized that I was not lying.

"Holy Mother of…Jaime?" he said and sat on the couch laughing. "How's life…you doing fine I see…our little business transaction turned out well for you!"

I could not believe his words! Even an animal cares for its offspring but Bill, was worse than an animal.

"How dare you ask me how's life? After everything you did to me, you have the guts to say those words to me…I told you you're lucky…I should blow your head off!" I yelled at him, and he got visibly scared when he thought I had a gun. I didn't, but I wish I had.

"Yo yo...relax baby, don't talk about shooting around here!" he said with a scared voice.

"Not a word! You don't get the privilege of talking right now! You don't have that right after you sold me as if I were a dog...right in the hands of the biggest pimp around! You know what happened to me after that? You probably could care less, but I'm gonna tell you anyway! Right from the very next day I was forced into prostitution, and it has been ongoing since the last time I saw you...but what would you know about that..." I basically screamed it in his face but he was still looking at me with a straight face, even smiling slightly from time to time.

"Oh hush, I would sign up right away if someone would pay me to have sex...so stop complaining so much!" he replied arrogantly... that was it!

"You heartless monster..." I yelled and jumped on top of him and started swinging for his face.

I did not care anymore that he was my biological father. To me he was just the sperm donor who ruined my life and was now laughing about it. In my mind, he deserved the worst possible and...it was about time he got it!

"This...is...what...you...get...for being...such scum!" I kept saying while punching him.

Tim heard the noise from outside...as things had gotten pretty violent. Bill on the other hand did not gasp while he was being hit... as if he did not even feel it at all and that drove me even madder.

Bill's was lucky that Tim came in and grabbed me, otherwise who knows if I would have ever stopped!

"You're crazy like your momma...you belong in a nut house!" he replied as soon as he regained his composure.

"I'll show you crazy..." I said while trying to break free from Tim's grip.

"It's not worth it..." Tim whispered to me and this helped me breathe normally again.

All of a sudden, a woman came out of the bedroom screaming. She was half-naked and looking like she had just came out of a trash bin.

"Who are you people…what are you doing in my living room…get out of here, right now before I call the cops!" she screamed menacingly but I was not scared of her. I just did not understand who she was and what she was doing there. My first question to Bill was, "Where is my mother?"

"She's dead, committed suicide a few years back…not my fault." Bill replied nonchalantly and this time I really wanted to kill him.

"Say that again?" I asked again as I could not believe it.

"She dead…this is my new headache…say hello to Genevieve!" he laughed again.

"What is wrong with you man?" I replied and was one step from punching him again.

His 'new headache' stepped in.

"Stay away from my man…you whore…"

"What did you call me?" I turned my head towards her with anger "I'll slap those nasty looking teeth out of your mouth if you open it again!"

Seeing that tension was overflowing, Tim stepped in to calm the situation.

"Back off…Jamie wants nothing to do with this low life." he said to her, but the she was getting even angrier.

"What did you call him?" she yelled at Tim who was just looking at her.

"You…shut your trap!"

"Now Bill, what did you say happened to mom? Why?" I asked him again. My blood was boiling in my veins and my body was shaking all over. I could barely control myself…I was glad that Tim was there with me.

"I told you she killed herself…what else do you want to know? I guess she felt guilty for what happened to you…she tried to find you, but she had no luck, so she woke up one day and over dosed…what do I know?" he replied with a relaxed voice as if he was depicting some TV show.

"I'm gonna kill you!" I yelled trying to break free from Tim's grip who would not let me go.

"Yeah right..." Bill laughed in my face "And this is how I got to keep all the money; happy ending!"

Tim could barely hold me, and Genevieve saw that. She suddenly felt the need to protect 'her man'... if Bill could ever be defined as such.

"If you come at him one more time, I will make you regret it... you hear me?" she said pointing her finger at me as if I was supposed to be afraid.

I turned my head towards her in disgust and spit right in her face with no warning. She lost it and tried to attack me.

"You dirty tramp..." she yelled and charged towards me, but she forgot that Tim was by my side...and he was a real man!

Tim did not miss a beat, he palmed Genevieve right in the face pushing her straight to the ground. She started crying but Bill did not even flitch; he was not even looking at 'his new headache'.

I leaned towards him as he was sitting relaxed on the couch... but as I got closer he got scared thinking probably that I may still have that gun.

"You are a low life scum and you deserve the worst for the rest of your days on this earth! I came here hoping to forgive you and my mother, but I don't know if that is possible. At least she had some type of remorse for what she did but you...

"Ohh yeah...w..." Bill tried to say but Tim stopped him right there.

"If I were you, I would keep my mouth shut...otherwise, you'll be next!" Tim said

Bill understood the message and stopped talking. He sat still only looking between us and his new headache. As for me, I had no reasons to be there anymore...it was over.

"Come on Jaime, let's get out of here, there's nothing good for you in this place!" Tim whispered and grabbed my shoulder.

"You're right...let's go" I replied and leaned my head on his shoulder. We both left the apartment and I swore never to look back. My mother is gone and as far as I'm concerned Bill is too!

I felt sorry for my mother and even if I was grieving, there was nothing more I could do. It was clear that Bill was heartless through all of it, but I decided to let fate deal with him and the consequences of his actions would eventually catch up with him. I had too much on my plate already.

"I'm sorry you had to go through all of that." Tim tried to comfort me as we were heading back to his motorcycle.

"It's fine don't worry" I mumbled "I had to do this…it's better that I dealt with it. I hate living with all those 'what if's' in my head; now I'm good and can go on with my life!" I replied but I did not really have a life to go on with.

I buried my head in his chest and sobbed deeply…Tim embraced me.

"It's okay…we're getting away from this place and never looking back!" he said but there was something else bothering me.

"I know…but it's not that," I said with a saddened voice, "it's…I can't do this anymore…this lie of a life; sometimes I feel like I am falling and can never reach the bottom" and I started crying. My eyes were flooded with tears that could not hold back anymore.

"That's not true" he replied with a kind voice "You're so young and have so much waiting for you; you have your whole life ahead of you!"

"What life? This? I don't want it anymore…" I mumbled while still crying.

"You know, you don't have to continue doing this if you don't want to, right?" he added and my eyes widened all of a sudden. I looked up at him with hope.

"You think I don't want that?" I replied "I dream of it most nights but wake up to the same nightmare every morning; I wish I could disappear one day and never come back. We both know that if I try to escape they will kill me. Going to the cops is not an option either because they are all linked with Mayor Simon and some of them are clients… I'm at a dead end with nowhere to go."

Tim looked at me for a couple of moments in silence.

"Then let me protect you, I can get you out of this safely."

"I won't allow you to get any more involved" I mumbled sadly "I roped you in far enough already…after all, you are my friend!"

"You're right about the friend part, but I see something in you and I know that you're better than all of this. Even with your crazy upbringing, you still manage to shine in this dark world of yours… this isn't something you find every day." he replied.

I buried my head back into his chest. "Tina does not trust you… you know that right?"

"Can't say that I blame her. I have not lead an exemplary life; I'm full of flaws but I'm working on most them. This is not about me or Tina…it's about you. You are a special soul with a lot of potential and I can't turn a blind eye to that…not anymore."

His words were kind and sweet and to some extent, they gave me a little bit of hope, but in the end they were just words and nothing more. I knew better what Bob and Francisco had in mind and how they would react if I ever dared to get out of line.

"I don't know, I am afraid that they would find me…and then that will be the end of me and anyone else that helped me." I said to him but Tim nodded negatively.

"I can get you out, I promise you that and no one will lay a finger on you…you have my word!" he said but I just could not believe that to be true.

"And how are you gonna do that?"

"My former gang has a safe haven outside the city, we're still family and I can set you up there…you will be safe. No one knows it exists, not even the cops." he added but it still sounded unreal to me.

"I…I can't and you know that…it's not that easy to just run away, and besides…there's Tina… I cannot leave her behind; I could not forgive myself!"

"I understand your point!" he said with a loud voice…and I could feel that he was getting agitated. "Look, I know that she is your friend, but you cannot go back there now, especially since they will know that you missed your appointment…you wanna get killed tonight?"

"I'll survive, but thanks for thinking about me." I replied and hugged him "You're the best, but I can't leave Tina behind, I just can't; she's been there with me from day one and we have both suffered, I have help her too."

"Fine then…but when are you planning to get out of there?" he asked and hugged me tightly.

"Tomorrow…they won't keep us late because we have to wake up early the next morning to get ready for church!"

Tim looked at me oddly…

"They some righteous pimps…aren't they? Do they think they can bribe God or something?"

I could not keep from laughing when looking at the expression on his face.

"I don't know…but let's leave that aside for now and focus on what we have to do." I replied but he was still picturing pimps going to church in his mind.

"Hey let's meet near the library down the street at 3 a.m., they'll be turning over in their sleep by then…we have a deal?" I asked and he nodded.

"Good…now I have to go!" I added but he would not let go.

"I don't wanna take you back to that snake bed" he replied. "You're safe now I have a bad feeling about you going back."

"I know…" I mumbled "but I have to go now, this is for the best."

"I won't drop you off there" he insisted.

"You don't have to…I don't want them to see you…drop me off somewhere along the road." I said and he agreed to that.

We left and he dropped me off a half a mile away from the house.

"Stay safe" he said to me "Library, 3a.m. sharp". I nodded and left.

I walked the rest of the distance, and as I got close to the house, I saw how Bob and Francisco came out screaming at each other. I instantly knew that this was about me and the fact that I missed my appointment with the mayor. Years before I would be scared to get closer when they were so mad, but at that time I did not care anymore…so I continued walking.

They spotted me eventually, so they ended their quarrel and focused their attention on me. Bob walked up to me looking like he was going to slap me.

"Where have you been?" he asked but I did not even look at him. My eyes were pointed at Francisco who stood next to the car.

"I went to see a doctor...I was not feeling well!" I replied and he raised his hand.

"Oh you're going to need a doctor in just a minute, you..."

"Bob...calm down!" Francisco yelled at him and he stopped.

"But she's clearly lying..." Bob replied.

"I said, calm down!" Francisco insisted.

"Whatever..." Bob mumbled and stepped to the side.

"Now Jaime, tell me what's wrong? And I don't want you to lie to me because I would hate to have you see my dark side. For all these years I have provided for you and treated you nicer than you have ever been treated...so, tell me, is that the truth?" Francisco asked looking straight at me. He did not even blink...not even once and that was pretty scary.

"You know I would never lie to you!" I replied and Francisco seemed to be pleased with my answer even if he still appeared to have a little bit of doubt.

"Fine then, it's settled!" he concluded and started walking towards the front door. Bob on the other hand was losing it.

"Unbelievable... now the girls tell us what's what!" he mumbled angrily.

Now Francisco started getting angry.

"Bob, not one more word...not one, do you hear me?" he said but Bob was still irritated and kept shaking his head.

Francisco turned his head towards me "You may go inside now and get some rest, we'll talk more in the morning!"

"Thank you" I replied and started walking towards the door.

Now, Francisco turned back and walked up to Bob. I had not gotten inside yet, so I managed to hear their little conversation.

"I can't believe it..." Bob kept grunting but Francisco got in his face angrier than I had ever seen him before.

"If you ever dare to disrespect me like that in front of her or any of the other girls, it will most certainly be your last time" and he grabbed Bob's neck. "I don't care that we have a long history together, you remember that you are living in my house and I am the one who allowed you to have this lifestyle. Don't let it go to your head…cause I'm still the boss around here!"

Francisco let go and they both walked separate ways. That was the first time I saw Francisco out of his usual calm state…and I was sure that was just a shade of his true dark side.

I was happy that I had gotten out of it unharmed, at least for the moment and went to my room. I found Tina sleeping on the bed, but I could not help waking her up to tell her all about it. I nudged her and she slowly opened her eyes.

"Jamie?" she asked with a sleepy voice.

"Shh, I'm back" I whispered so we did not make a fuss.

"You ok? What happened?" she asked as she was rubbing her eyes.

"Well, for starters you were right…"

"I'm so sorry…I didn't…"

"It's ok" I stopped her "It's not your fault anyway, come here" and we hugged for a moment.

"I was having such a horrible nightmare just now when you woke me up…" she said.

"How so?"

"Well, you were there in my dream, but you were not well at all… as matter of fact, you were lying in a pool of blood, almost beaten to death…it was so horrible, I don't even want to remember it!" she added and hugged me again.

"Don't worry, it's not going to happen…I told them I was not feeling well so I went to the emergency room, they're not gonna lay a hand on me" I replied and brushed her hair to the side. "Look at me, I'm gonna be fine…we're both gonna be…"

"I hope so," she mumbled "but it was so real!"

Our daily living nightmare had gotten under our skin so badly that even in our dreams we were riddled with fear and by the threat of sudden death if we ever dare to 'disrespect' Bob or Francisco. This had to change and I was not going to stop until I saw both of us away from that world of drugs, murders and sex.

"Look…we need to get out of here and live our own lives the way we want…we can't stay here anymore!" I said to her but she was still afraid.

"But how are we gonna…"

"Tim told me that there's a safe house that we can hide at…no one will ever find us, even the cops don't know a thing about that place…" I whispered because I did not want to be heard. Bob or Francisco could be lurking by our door at any time.

"But what if they find us? What then?" she stuttered.

"They won't, Tim will keep us safe! We're leaving tomorrow night and you're coming with me whether you like it or not."

"I wish it were so easy!" she smiled at me "I fear the worst will happen though…"

"I'd rather die than live another day like this…we're going!" I said.

For the first time I could say I was happy. A twisted kind of happiness mixed with fear, but it was something that managed to give me hope. After years of ongoing torture I could dream big again and dreaming big was good…I had almost forgotten what that felt like.

So the next day, I tried to act naturally, give them no reasons to be suspicious. Still Bob probably felt something was up because he started acting strangely. In the kitchen while having breakfast and in the hallway, he kept giving me that look…smiling at me as if he wanted to get in my good graces and ask me for a favor. Creepy.

And as I suspected, I woke up with him coming in my room that morning…wearing the same stupid smile on his face. Right then, I was sending Tim an email, so I hit send quickly and closed the laptop. I smiled back…fake smile of course.

"Hi Bob!" I said courteously.

"Jaime, I came here to apologize for last night…I overreacted!" he said with a 'sincere' voice but I could tell he was lying through his teeth.

"It's fine Bob, and it's my fault actually; I should have told you about it before taking action…I was just feeling so awful and totally forgot about the proper way to do things.

"I say we should put this behind us…forget about it!" he added and came to sit on the bed. I shuffled a few inches over…because I did not want to sit too close to him.

"I have an idea…" he started talking so I pretended to be interested.

"Let's hear it…"

"I was thinking to take you out to dinner tonight instead of working…what do you think? Just you and me, have a chat, patch some wounds…"

"And what about Francisco? What does he have to say about this?" I replied but Bob pushed his hand through the air.

"You don't have to worry about that, I handle my own business." he replied with the attitude of an oversized ego.

"As long as things are cool, I got nothing against it." I replied. He smiled at me and I smiled back.

"I'll meet you downstairs in an hour then?" he asked as he was about to leave my room.

"One hour is all that I need." I smiled and he winked at me closing the door from the exterior.

"Something's not right…" I thought to myself.

Five seconds later, Tina came in agitated.

"What was that all about? Bob's all smiling and everything" she asked curiously.

"He wants me to go to dinner with him this evening instead of working…" I replied lifting my shoulders. Tina was even more surprised than me.

"Whaat? Since when does Bob…"

"I have no clue but I'm sure he's up to something." I replied and started looking for something proper to wear to our surprise dinner.

"I guess you've had your last appointment then…" Tina smiles, but I could tell that she was still worried.

"Yeah…I guess."

"I'm scared…What if my dream was some sort of premonition?" she replied and I stopped her before she could say anything else.

"It's going to be ok, trust me! You just go to the meeting spot at three o' clock on the dot, with or without me, promise me!" I said and Tina almost started crying.

"What is the point of all of this if you're not going to be there? I don't want to do this alone; we are either getting away together or going down together. You're the one who made all this possible so you deserve to be there…you have to be there!"

"You know I will do my best to be there, don't worry, we'll both be fine." I said to her. Two seconds later her alarm goes on.

She sighs deeply "Ohh God, I have to go now, otherwise I'll be late for my appointment."

"Be brave…just one more and we'll be free." I tried to encourage her.

"Just one more." She smiled and headed out.

I had less than 30 minutes left to get ready now, so I grabbed the first nice dress I could lay my eyes on and slipped it on. I applied a little bit of make up and went downstairs to meet Bob. He was dressed as usual…nothing fancy, just a pair of jeans and a shirt.

"Where are we going?" I asked him as I was coming down the stairs.

"Changed my mind" he replied "why waste the good food we have around here, we'll be dining inside, I hope you're okay with that."

This was a sudden change… something was clearly not right, and I was soon going to learn all about it.

"I'm fine, dinner at home is as good as eating out." I said and he looked away.

"That's what I thought." he mumbled to himself.

I had wasted all my energy to dress up for nothing, and as I got in the dining room, I could see that on the table was the same old food we ate on a daily basis. Some chicken and vegetables plus a bottle of wine that was opened already.

We sat quietly at the table facing each other…and for some reason I felt uncomfortable. I lost my appetite with all that tension in the air, but I had to eat something because I knew that Bob would have one of those 'ungrateful brat' type reactions.

With all my efforts, I did not manage to dodge his angry eyes and nasty attitude.

"So, how's the food?" he asked me all of a sudden while we were eating.

"It's good as always…" I replied while trying not to choke on that chicken.

"It is good, isn't it?" he smiled at me "Life here is good right?"

"It is, and I am very appreciative for what you guys have done for me." I thanked him, but he did not seem to be pleased with my answer.

"Jaime, do you take me for a fool?"

"You want me to tell the truth?" I replied trying not to sound sarcastic.

"I would like that very much!" he said with the voice of a wanna be gentleman.

I looked straight at him for a couple of moments while he was still eating and peeking at me from time to time.

"I appreciate the opportunity you have given me, what else can I say?" I replied and went back to my eating.

Bob scowled at me for a few brief moment, then his face relaxed all of a sudden.

"Hmm, then I am assuming that you are feeling a lot better now, right?"

"I'm ok." I replied trying to avoid any conflict, but Bob was just getting started.

"That's funny, you think? Because last night you acted like you almost died and had to go to the emergency room…and now, you're just fine, miraculously! You're quite the miracle case, aren't you?" he replied sarcastically.

"What can I say, I'm no doctor?" I replied with a straight face "It was probably a short lived bug…"

"Alright…" he laughed "then what did the doctor say? What was wrong with you that disappeared so miraculously?"

"I was having severe stomach pains, he wasn't sure what is was…" I said and left the fork on the table "I thought this was an apology dinner but I see that I am subject of a cross examination; may I be excused? I am not hungry anymore."

"Wait a minute" he hollered at me and slammed his fork on the table. "I'm not done yet!"

I did not eat anymore, and just sat there and looked at him. He grabbed his fork and started eating again slowly.

"You know that I just wanna make sure that you are okay…if you're sick it's bad for business, and what's bad for business is bad for all of us." He added and grabbed his glass.

"Here's to your good health and well-being! You're fortunate to have both…may you be as happy from now on as you have been so far." he said smiling but I was disgusted by his theatrical act by now.

I just sat there watching him goof around. It was clear that his real intention had been shown yet and I was wondering what he was going to do next.

"You know it's bad luck not to raise the glass when someone is giving a toast, right?" he insisted I raised my glass.

"No I didn't" I replied and grabbed my glass because I knew he would not give up until I did it.

"May you always have everything you desire…including health and wellbeing!" he finally ended so I could leave. We both sipped from our glasses and I left with him applauding as I walked off.

With every passing moment, I grew more and more anxious as I knew the crucial moment was getting closer. For the rest of that evening I could not sleep a wink, so I just read a book and kept checking my email and every once in a while I would glance at the clock to see how much time was left.

I packed a couple of essentials in a small bag and tried to find the perfect outfit for my escape. I knew that I would remember those clothes for the rest of my life. I took a black pair of jeans on and a dark shirt; as I was looking in the mirror, I observed that a piece of it was still missing. It was half past 2 a.m. and we needed to get moving.

Tina quietly crawled over to my room.

"S'up girl, you ready?" I asked her full of hope.

"Do I have a choice?" she replied and stood with her back against the door.

"It's gonna be alright, a few more minutes and we are out of this prison." I whispered trying to comfort her. She was visibly scared and her hands were shaking.

I did not get to finish my words completely when Tina felt the door being pushed against her back.

Chapter 6

The fight of my life

SHE GASPED. OUR EYES WIDENED AS IT WAS CLEAR THAT someone was trying to get in.

The door got pushed again, more violently this time… it was Bob!

"You ladies planning on going somewhere so early in the morning?" he said displaying the same old smirk on his face. "Sorry for the interruption."

"We are not going anywhere." Tina replied but Bob had a different agenda in mind.

"The hell you aren't…" he laughed, "not now that I have caught you in the middle of it."

"You see, I knew you were up to something, you little ingrate" he said and started pointing at me. "You may have Francisco fooled, but I knew you stopped fearing us a long time ago."

I knew I should have played the nice girl, but I could not take it anymore, so I said it!

"You're right I am not afraid of you anymore…you ain't nothing to me!"

"Ohh, is that right?" he reacted and started rubbing his hands "Well let me prove otherwise and show you how things really are in this house!"

Tina was so scared and did not know what to do. With Bob right next to the door, it looked like there was no escape for us.

"Jaime" she stuttered and looked at me. I managed to keep it together and was planning the next move. It was clear to me it was going to be him or us.

"We're fine Tina…don't worry!" I replied but looking at Bob the whole time.

"Fine?" Bob laughed "Ohh you're not fine at all Tina, and you know why? I'm gonna beat the fear back into both of you and then I'm gonna have my way with you while your crawling on the floor… that's what I'm gonna do! It's time you two were put in your place!"

This had to end! One way or another, so I grabbed my bag tightly and waited for the perfect moment. Tina kept looking at me…then out of the blue, I swing my bag and hit Bob right above his eyes.

"Ruunn" I screamed but Tina looked like she was paralyzed. "Ruuun for your life!" and she finally ran out. With Bob dizzy now, I charged him and drove him into the wall. Now all I had to do was make it out of there, but he grabbed my ankle and I fell. I kicked him as hard as I could, but when he got anrgy he became even stronger.

Bob got up before I could and closed the door trapping me inside the room.

"Now I got you all to myself…and I'm about to enjoy every moment of this."

I was trapped and it looked like this was going to be the end of me…but all of a sudden, I remembered that shard of glass under my mattress from all those years ago. I lunged to the corner of the bed and grabbed it…

Now Bob stormed towards me trying to grab me, but I ducked and stabbed him in the leg with it…

"You little piece of!" he screamed while falling on the floor.

"This is it!" I thought to myself "This is where he dies!" and raised my weapon above my head ready to give him the final blow.

He pulled a gun from the small of his back and pointed it straight in my face!

"You thought you were going to kill me? I'm sorry but it's not your lucky day." He said to me while screaming with pain.

"Put it down!"

"I won't!"

"Put that glass down before I blow your head off!" he yelled at me but I was not willing to give up that easily.

"NO!" I screamed back and lunged at him trying to hit him again. I knew he would not shoot me, I was too valuable for them.

Unfortunately, he dodged my attack and managed to knock me to the ground. The shard of glass flew out of my hand landing on the floor, and when I tried to get my hands on it he threw himself on top me and pinned me to the floor.

"You ain't going nowhere…it's time I taught you a little lesson!" he said and while banging my head against the floor.

I struggled to break free, but he was too heavy, and when he realized that I was reaching for the shard, he hit me in the head with the butt of the gun. I almost lost it but I struggled to stay conscious. I screamed as loud as I could as he was hitting me violently.

"You ain't never gonna leave this place…you hear that? You'll die screwing for money!"

By now I was somewhere in between this world and the next one. I could not feel my body or breathe normally anymore and every second seemed like an eternity to me. Eventually I abandoned myself into his hands, as I did not have any energy to fight back. He turned me around and started hitting me in the face as hard as he could…with his gun…I wasn't feeling anything anymore…and I might as well be dead; it did not matter anymore.

By now, my face felt like it had a thousand needles stuck into it; everything was so numb and I could barely grasp reality. I was sure that I was going to die in that room, but God sent Francisco who entered the room right as Bob was about to finish me off.

"What in the world are you doing man?!" he yelled at Bob who was breathing heavily.

"She was trying to run away, just like I told you she would…Tina already ran!" he said and Francisco looked in the hallway.

"And as a punishment you decided to kill her?"

""I ain't kill nobody…she's still alive!" Bob replied as he kicked me for proof.

"Yeah right…but she will be soon enough…you know we can't take her to the hospital like this!"

"So what…" Bob replied satisfied by his deeds.

"We don't have time to argue over this…put her in the trunk of my car!" Francisco ordered Bob.

"Why?"

"Just do it, now!" Francisco yelled at him.

Bob then grabbed my limp body and threw it over his shoulder. I could feel the room spinning around me. I could barely see where he was taking me as my eyes were swollen and filled with blood.

As he was carrying me on his shoulder, we passed by a room which had the door open. A little girl around the age of seven came out to see what was going on. She had probably been awakened by the violent noises. She looked at me as I was being carried away…her pretty brown eyes were probably traumatized by the scene she was witnessing.

By now, I began come out of that extreme numbness and I could feel every part of my body throbbing in pain; especially my face and my chest. When Bob reached Francisco's car, he opened the trunk and threw me in as if I were a sack of potatoes.

I gasped as I did not have the energy to scream. Francisco appeared moments later and came to look at me.

"Close the trunk and I don't want to hear a word from you…I don't even wanna hear you breathe! Got that?" he said to Bob who kept looking at me with a smirk on his face. "Now get in the car! I don't have all night!"

When Bob closed the trunk, it all got dark and I felt like I was in hell. There was a nasty smell in there and I could not tell what it was. Then this crazy idea came to mind that I was not the first girl who got this treatment from them. It looked like they had preset procedures for this type of event.

I had lost track of time by now and it seemed like I had been there in the darkness for an eternity. Eventually, the car stopped and I could hear something. I could not define it exactly…and only when Francisco opened the trunk did I realized the sounds was rushing water, we were close to a river.

They stood up there, dressed all in black with black gloves.

"Get her out of the trunk" said Francisco and Bob leaned and grabbed me by the neck and legs. "Now let's go!"

They carried me to the edge of the river, and stood there for a couple of moments. Both Bob and Francisco looked in the distance probably trying to see if there was anyone nearby.

"Now what?" Bob asked "Should we throw her in?"

"Yeah…but we need to make sure she's dead." Francisco replied and pulled out his gun. At that moment, I was sure I was gonna die.

Bob did not doubt Francisco for a second and tried to throw me into the cold water of the river, but as he was getting on is knee, Francisco aimed right in the back of Bob's head and fired twice. Bob died instantly and we both fell in the water, and I nearly drowned as Bob's body was pressing onto mine. I wanted to scream for help but I did not have the energy for it.

Francisco quickly threw himself in the water and pulled me out letting Bob go with the waves.

"Jaime, Jaime…come back to me!" he screamed "I'm so sorry this happened to you!" I wished I could answer but my mouth was filled with water. Even so, I was confused by this sudden change…and did not know what to believe anymore.

"I never wanted for such things to happen" Francisco continued "I took pride in protecting you from this evil world of ours…but failed to protect you from the one who was right under my nose. I'm so sorry!"

He leaned towards me and kissed me on the forehead. Blood was stuck on his lips as my whole face was covered by a mixture of dry blood and dirty river water.

Now I could see him grab his gun again… with tears in his eyes.

"I love you Jaime…with all my heart you were always the most beautiful to me and I cannot have you suffer like this anymore!"

His love now meant putting me out of my misery…what a noble gesture, but I did not want to die even if I was suffering greatly. He pointed his gun to my head. I could see the barrel between my eyes… and I wanted to cry, but I could not do it anymore…I just waited for the last shot.

By now, I was talking to God in my mind asking for forgiveness and a way out. I guess He heard my cry because right as Francisco was about to pull the trigger, a light started shining nearby.

"This is my angel coming for me!" I thought to myself thinking I was dead already, but it was not actually an angel…maybe one in disguise.

"Who's out there?" the voice of a man asked. "Come out…I have a shotgun!"

Francisco started panicking, and ran back to his car. He knew that if someone would see him there with me, he would end up in jail for the rest of his life.

The man scanned the landscape with his flashlight and looked around to see if he could spot the origin of the noise. I started splashing the water with my right hand…that was all I was able to do. My voice was gone and I could not scream for help.

I could see Francisco in the distance how he looked at me for the last time, then got in his car and drove away.

Soon enough, the old man spotted me. I had been left to drown but God had other plans.

"Ohh you poor soul, what happened to you? Who is the beast that did this to you?" he said with a worried voice while dragging me out of the cold water.

"Oh my God, you look awful!" he added. "Who could be so cold hearted to abandon you here?"

He grabbed me in his arms the best way he could and took me to his truck. I could tell he was an older man and struggled slightly to carry me.

"You need immediate care…otherwise we'll lose you!" he mumbled and started driving. The sun had started to rise by now, and I feared that this was going to be my last sunrise.

After looking at the sun for a couple of moments, my eyes grew tired and I blacked out. I did not remember anything from that moment on, and I have no idea how long I had been out.

Chapter 7

Love that is stronger than blood

WHEN I FINALLY OPENED MY EYES AGAIN, I FOUND myself in a nice bed covered with soft white linens. I was covered in bandages but my wounds didn't look fresh.

"Oh God, how long have I been out?" I thought to myself while looking around. I did not recognize the room and wondered where I was then I realized that I was probably in the house of that nice old man who had saved me.

As I turned my head, I saw this older lady who was carrying a pillow. She dropped it when she saw me looking at her.

"Kevin…Kevin come quick!" she screamed.

"What is it Liz?" the old man asks as he was getting close to the door.

"She's awake!" she replied with tears in her eyes.

"Where am I?" I asked confused as they got closer.

"You're safe now honey, you don't have to worry about a thing!" Kevin said.

"Where is Tina?" I mumbled.

They looked at each other confused.

"I only found you there that night…there was no one else." Kevin added. I was shocked to hear that.

"No one else?" I pondered.

They looked at each other a couple of times; they were confused and probably scared too.

"Honey, we want to help you." Elizabeth sat closer to me. "Do you remember anything so we can go to the police?"

I said no… I knew that the police would not help in any way. Heck, if the wrong policeman heard my story it might get back to Francisco, some of them were his clients after all.

"Where are we?" I asked them but they were reluctant in telling me. I glanced out the window and as far as my eyes could see were these beautiful green hills.

"How were you involved in this situation…" Kevin said with an inquisitive tone.

I gasped…"Could you tell me please?"

"About 50 miles north of the city." he replied. "Why are you so concerned?"

"I am afraid that you were followed." I replied and the look as his face changed suddenly.

"Followed by who? I don't think anyone came after us? As long as you refuse to tell us what happened to you, I don't know if we can help," he replied and I felt the need to confess. They had been more than kind to me, and deserved to know the truth.

They both drew closer to me and placed their hands on my shoulders.

"You can tell us whatever you are comfortable with" Elizabeth added with the kindest voice I had ever heard in my life. "No one will judge you here or condemn you for anything."

"Ohh God, I don't even know what to begin with." I replied and they both smiled at me.

I started telling them about my parents and how they used me, with all the traumas and drama and then about Francisco and Bob and how I was sold to them for $10,000. To Kevin and Elizabeth, my confessions seemed like something out of a movie and the more I told them the more their eyes widened. I had suffered more in 18 years of life than most people suffer in 80 years, if at all.

"This is some life story! I have a lot more years behind me than I do ahead of me, but I never heard of such things until now!" Kevin replied.

"And that's not all!" I added and they both shook their heads.

"Poor souls" Elizabeth concluded.

"Wouldn't you like something to eat, you must be starving!" Kevin interrupted to break up the intensity of the moment. "Elizabeth here is the greatest cook the world has ever seen!"

"Oh stop it, you are exaggerating," she giggled "You're so flattering…as always!"

This image warmed my heart. Seeing two people who have lived together for almost 40 years and still loving each other like it was the first day. I had never seen anything like it.

"I'll go fix you something, the food is almost ready." Elizabeth said and exited the room in a rush. Kevin followed her.

Fifteen minutes later I heard someone knocking at the door; it was Elizabeth.

"It's done honey…you can come to the dining room, it's better when it's warm!" she said smiling.

I was starving no doubt, but I had not gotten out of the bed thus far and forgot about the pain. I tried to jump out of it as I used to do, but my ribs reminded me that they had been brutalized. I held my breath for a minute and got up like an old woman…inch by inch and holding the edge of the bed with both my hands.

"You need help?" she asked me concerned but I said no. I could do this, after all, I had managed to beat death…so this should be a piece of cake…in theory at least.

"I'll be there in a minute." I replied but she still looked worried.

I could smell something wonderful from down the hall, and soon enough I got to meet Elizabeth's famous turkey stew. It looked and tasted absolutely delicious, and combined with my hunger…well, I just started shoveling in.

"Slow down honey!" Elizabeth smiled at me. "I've made plenty!"

Everything was so good and I just could not stop eating. My stomach felt like it was a bottomless pit. I felt like I could have eaten anything that looked like food.

As I was sitting at the table, I saw Kevin getting close with an old laptop in his hands. He smiled at me…

"No promises, but I think we can make this antique work so you can contact your friend." he said and handed it to me. I opened the laptop…and it was indeed pretty old.

I turned it on and checked my emails to see if I had any from Tim or Tina and I had quite a few of them. They were both worried, and in the last one they wrote to me that they feared I was lost for good. Also, it looked like Tina met Tim that night and she was doing pretty well at the moment. She was being tutored by Ryan, who was Tim's friend and also an educator; this way Tina could get her degree and start a new life.

I answered a couple of them and told Tim and Tina briefly a few things about my current situation and most importantly that I was still ALIVE!

"Such great news!" I exclaimed and burst in tears as I kept reading.

"What is it dear?" Kevin asked curiously.

"My friend Tina is doing great and she's being tutored right now… this way she'll be able to get out of that life!"

"Well, that's great news Jaime!" Elizabeth stepped in closer, "You know, I could tutor you too if you wanted…I can teach you myself… well only if you choose to stay with us, of course!"

My eyes widened and I could not believe that these two people were offering to treat me as their own. Their words were indeed strange to me…after all the people who were supposed to love and care for me were willing to sell me for money, but by some twist of fate God has placed me with two strangers that are willing to help me without asking for anything in return?

"That would be like…a dream come true to me." I said timidly while tears of joy were rolling down my face. "I can't thank you both enough!"

"You don't have to." Kevin said standing up "You don't owe us anything…as a matter of fact, it is our pleasure to have you here."

Before I even knew what I was doing, I had rushed toward him and hugged him tightly.

"Thank you, thank you so much!" I said nervously.

"You're gonna be just fine with us!" Kevin replied as he embraced me back. "You'll see!"

Kevin, left out to do some work on the ranch and I thanked Elizabeth for the wonderful meal then I went back to my room because I was still exhausted. My body was aching pretty badly and as strong as I wanted to be, I could not do much other than eat and rest.

Eating that good stew, caused me to become sleepy, and as soon as I laid on the bed my eyes grew tired and I took a nap for a couple of hours.

Waking up, I realized it was dark outside. I turned on the lights and spotted a picture on the dresser. I picked it up and looked at it… the girl in the picture was absolutely beautiful. Her facial features and body proportions were perfect.

"My face will never be pretty like this again!" I thought to myself as I looked in the mirror.

The lacerations were steal healing and I could still feel the pain.

I asked God how He could allow that to happen to me… now I was marked for life. I knew that I had to move forward as a new person… to me, the old Jaime died at the river and now I had to try to find my new identity. Every morning since I've been there Kevin would ask my the same question"Tell me why you're beautiful?" I could never give him an honest answer so I would just look at the floor, waiting for the awkward moment to pass.

A knock at the door. As I turned around with the photo in my hand, I could see Kevin. I put the picture back on the dresser quickly.

"Sorry, I didn't…" I tried to say but Kevin interrupted me.

"No need to apologize."

I turned my head and took another look at the photo.

"She's Annabelle, our daughter…" he replied.

"She is so beautiful" I added and he smiled.

"Aha…now…tell me why you're beautiful?" he asked again and this time it just felt different.

"I…wish I could." I said looking down at the floor.

I sat on the bed and he came to sit next to me.

"You see, Annabelle was about your age in that picture…" he gasped…and I did not know why at first.

"Will I ever get to meet her?" I asked with the innocence of a person who did not know the full story.

Kevin looked at me and I could read sadness in his eyes.

"Oh I wish you could," he replied somberly, "so badly…I am sure you two would have hit it off really well; you have the same fire in your eyes as she used to have!"

When hearing the word 'used' I knew that something was wrong. Kevin turned towards me with tears in his eyes.

"She died shortly after this picture was taken. It's a total mirage, she looks so happy and smiling on the outside, when in fact she was screaming for help on the inside. Annabelle got involved with the wrong people and started doing drugs…a little bit of pot at first then it was the pain pills and she just kept spiraling downward after that. We found her one morning lying on her back, foam coming from her mouth, her face was pale…she had been dead for hours and we didn't even know."

I could not believe it, that picture looked so alive…but I guess looks can be deceiving. I had been playing that game myself without even knowing it. Playing the part of the strong girl that doesn't feel anything and isn't bothered by the things that have happened to her but inside it was eating away at me; it was a lie.

"I'm so sorry Kevin" I said trying to comfort him but his tears kept rolling down.

Kevin grabbed the picture and looked at her.

"You know, she could never tell me why she was beautiful whenever I asked her. She would always look at the floor and wait for me to leave and all I could see was a beautiful young girl…but that was just the surface. She was never able to unlock her beauty on the inside and that was what ultimately destroyed her."

I was speechless, and all I could do was be there for him. Kevin grabbed my hand and looked into my eyes.

"Never forget that your beauty lies within and it must be unlocked to work its way to the outside." he said. "You are beautiful because you are unique, because you are fearfully and wonderfully made, despite all that you may have been through you still have a lot of laughing and living to do. You're meant to do great things in this life and we are going to help you to the best of our ability to get there!"

I started crying myself... "Thank you" I replied, and he tightened his grip on my hand.

"As I told you already...you don't have to thank me, not ever!" he insisted and hugged me. As I was sitting there I could see my face in the mirror and could not help but think of his words...beauty had multiple facets in this world, he was right about that...If I could just unlock that thing inside I would start to feel worthy and beautiful, even with my wounds.

After that night, I decided to stay with the Smiths. Kevin and Elizabeth were great people and cared for me as if I were their own child. In their home I felt loved and appreciated and I also managed to find my self- worth.

Chapter 8

From much pain came great purpose

A FEW YEARS LATER, KEVIN DIED FROM HEART complications, but lived to see me walk across the stage and receive my law degree. At the ceremony he said to me "now I can die a happy man" and smiled at me like the world's proudest dad.

Time had passed and I had mostly healed from the terrible ordeals of my past. But even though I felt strong and in a much better place, I began to think of the other girls that were in the same predicament, those that weren't so lucky to escape as I had. In particular, the face of that young girl that I saw as Bob carried my limp body out of the house to the car trunk begin to haunt me, night after night. Finally, I resolved that I had to do something about it.

With the help of Elizabeth, Tina, Tim, and Ryan we put a plan together to get her out of there and it went off without a hitch. That single act of fearlessness lit a fire that consumed us all…we discovered our purpose which was to help young girls who had not been so fortunate in life…girls just like me and Tina, who had been thrown into the clutches of vicious pimps, girls whose parents did not care enough to protect them…with us they would find a sanctuary.

Five years have passed since that first rescue mission and yet I was still the same…still a little scared but hopeful. Somehow my past experiences had prepared me for my destiny…if it were not for my own misfortunes, so many lives would not have been touched in a positive way. Who knew that from pain could be drawn so much happiness and hope.

It was morning and I was looking in the mirror. The scars were less visible. Every day I would touch them with my finger to make sure they were still there; this way I knew it wasn't a dream; I had survived.

A car noise could be heard in the distance, so I moved a bit to the right and looked through the window. I rushed downstairs to see what this was all about. I did not get to reach the middle of the stairs before Elizabeth greeted me.

"Morning, Jaime" and then the rest of the girls who were eating already greeted me in unison.

"Moooorrningg Jaimeee!" I smiled.

"Morning everyone…how's breakfast huh?"

"Awesomee" they all screamed…and they were telling the truth, Elizabeth was such an awesome cook.

I walked up to Elizabeth who was doing the dishes.

"I think our next arrival is here…I saw the car getting close," I said to her.

She left the dishes in the sink and dried her hands. "Ok then, "she replied "I'll take the girls over to Ryan for their lessons!"

"Thank you so much!" I whispered and left.

When I finally reached out, Tim had pulled up the car and opened the back doors.

"She's in pretty bad shape!" she said to me as she was getting closer. "She's young too, probably in her lower teens!"

"Poor thing!" I said as I looked at the poor girl.

"Her name is Judith." Tim added "She's still sedated, but she should wake up any minute now."

"Let's get her inside." I said and we both grabbed her feeble body. She was lighter than a feather.

Tina was there with me, and as Tim took Judith up in his arms we got a little time to chit chat.

"You know it's been 5 years since we started doing this…saving these girls who were exactly like us…I feel like one of those super heroes in the movies!" she said to me.

"I didn't know you were keeping count…" I replied.

"How couldn't I? It's a celebration, a milestone and I think we should do something nice for the girls!" she said and I could not agree more.

"They would love that!" I said "I can't believe we're doing this sometimes."

"Tell me about it…" Tina mumbled.

"When I think about how bad we started out and where life eventually took us, I don't think I would have it any other way if it were for me to choose again. I got to meet you, and Tim and these great people who are helping us and look at how we are able to help these girls!"

We decided to build a long stage in one of the old barns on the property and called it the "Walk of Beauty" and it was set up like a runway. All of us accept Tim and Ryan of course, would walk this runway one at a time and everyone else would be seated or standing on either side. Ryan would be the DJ playing some runway music and they would all be screaming "Tell my why you're beautiful!" in unison and on beat. Whenever the girl would approach the end of the runway she would have to answer with attitude. They all would have so much fun doing this. It would help some to break out of their shell and gave others a boost of confidence. It was also an attempt to break the mind-set of what they were brainwashed to believe beauty was when they were trapped in sex trafficking.

When we got to Judith's room, she was awake already and looking around, probably confused because she did not know what was happening to her.

"How are you feeling?" I asked her and sat next to her on the bed.

"Okay I guess," she replied "All I can remember is leaving my father's house, I blacked out after that and woke up here!"

"You're safe now, don't worry!" I said to her and caressed her hand. "Judith, can I ask you a question? Was your father forcing you to sleep with men for money?"

"He did not make me do it…I wanted to." she replied and I was shocked to hear it. These poor kids were so messed up that they did not even know that they were being used and manipulated.

"You're too young to call sex 'consensual' and the fact that your father was getting paid for what he made you do makes it illegal!" Tim intervened and only confused Judith even more.

"I know it was wrong," she said "but it made him happy, and the men…"

I was stupefied by the words coming out of the mouth of this young girl. Judith had been brainwashed since birth. Scared and confused she had never been taught her true worth.

She looked around with a panicked look on her face.

"You have to take me back…otherwise, they'll kill me if they know I'm gone!"

I shook my head in disapproval and she could not understand why I had this attitude.

"You know, Tina and I were in the same situation as you, forced for years to have sex with strange men, sold from hand to hand, but we escaped and managed to save all of these girls you see here; they're fine now and we could do the same for you."

"I'm afraid he will find me…and then…" she replied and I understood her fear.

"He won't honey…we'll make sure that you're safe and well."

"Are you sure?" she asked again. I could see that she was terrified.

"I swear I won't let anything bad happen to you." I said to her while holding her hands.

"Okay then." Judith replied.

Elizabeth entered the room holding a plate of one of her delicious dishes. It smelled great as always and Judith noticed that quickly.

"This looks great!" she said.

"And it's all for you!" Elizabeth said smiling.

"Thank you!" Judith replied and grabbed the plate. She was obviously hungry.

I brushed her hair gently with my hand. "Eat up…we'll go now and give you some privacy and time to rest. Tomorrow we'll introduce you to the rest of the girls if you feel up to it." I told her as we all prepared to leave the room.

Judith nodded in approval.

"That's great Judith" I smiled and left. By now she had grabbed the fork and started eating.

The next morning, I walked outside to this spot on the ranch where there girls were having class. There is a patch of grass under this large oak tree where Tim taught the girls how to defend themselves in case someone attacked them. He thought this to be necessary because of the world the girls had come from and also as a way of returning their power to them.

I passed by and saw each of the girls taking their turn at the drill. They were both happy and focused at the same time. It was essential that we had a powerful strategy to build the girls up because they have certainly been broken down. I made sure that me and Tina shared our story with them so that they knew that we are from the same or similar circumstance as them. Now it was time for me to speak to the class before Ryan does his magic because he is a tough act to follow.

I address the class, "You know for a very long time I battled in my mind if God was real and my main argument was if He was real, why would He allow so many awful things to happen to me? Why would He allow me to be born to parents that were strung out on meth? Why would he allow me to be sold to a pimp at age 13, one that actually treated me a lot better than my parents did, but still made me sleep with men for money? Why would he allow me to be beaten and left for dead leaving my face covered in scars? I used to ask all of these questions over and over and I didn't begin to receive the answers until the Smiths came into my life. When they took me in and begin raising me as their own daughter I knew that there was a God. I could clearly see God in them, but when I look into all of your eyes I can see why God allowed me to go through hell, it prepared me to be able to understand exactly what you all have been through. So that I could help you to believe that you were never abandoned by God. Most of us were victims of bad decisions and consequences even if they weren't our own. The reality is that children often have to suffer for the mistakes of their parents, but the good news is that even though we may not get to determine how your story began it doesn't mean that we can't decide how our story will end. You also have the opportunity to break the cycle simply by unlocking the beauty on the inside of you and transforming into who God intended for you to be. God knew who you were meant to be before you were even formed in your mother's womb. Now this can be a very long and intense journey but you all have been through the worse of it and you deserve to experience the freedom and love that will come as a result of this path and as a result of your work to heal yourself. Not to mention your future children will greatly benefit in so many ways from your transformation as they will receive the good start that we did not get."

One of the girls, Erica, raised her hand. I could look in her eyes and tell that she was struggling with what was just said, "I want to believe that what you are saying is real and even possible for me, but I have only known one thing my whole life and that is sleeping with men for money and getting with the best pimp for protection. If God is real He should've come and visited the area I was working in. I'm not sure what unlocking this "beauty" will do for me because I have been called beautiful by so many different man more times than I could count, but what has that really done for me? I was still used and abused at will. I was probably treated worse because my pimp always expected me to bring in the most money and the other girls treated me badly because they felt like I was shown favoritism. I don't want to be beautiful because beauty has brought me nothing but pain." She burst into tears. A few of the other girls went over to console her and Elizabeth walked into the room when she heard the outburst.

Elizabeth took the floor, "Okay girls I want you all to come with me. We are about to go to the 'Wall of Beauty'." The Wall of Beauty was an entire wall that was one long mirror from floor to ceiling. Me and Elizabeth began handing all of the girls post-its.

Elizabeth continued, "Now I want you all to pick a spot in the mirror and stare at your reflection deep and hard. Write down at least three things that you see about yourself and be honest. The truth that you are bold enough to admit today will lead you to the truth that will one day set you free." All of the girls looked at each other and one by one begin to write. Sadness and tears begin to fill the room.

I then added, "There is no right or wrong thing to write here just let it come from the heart." Erica yelled out "I hate what I see and I don't want to do this and you can't make me." Elizabeth goes over to her. "This is for your benefit you have to trust the process, but I can promise you that things will only get better from here. In time you will come and look into this same spot and you will see something different. You will see what we all see and most importantly what God sees. This will also help you to let it out and let it go. Whatever you see just write it and place it on the wall right in front of you. This room is covered with love and no one will be allowed to judge you." Elizabeth gently rubs her back. "Come on." Erica timidly replies, "Okay."

Next we went back to the classroom and Ryan begins telling his story which never fails to grab the attention of the entire room.

"Morning, I'm Ryan most of you already know my story but a few of you don't. As far back as I can remember I wanted to educate, motivate, and inspire others. As a child I would get up and try to teach the class whenever the teacher would step out. I went on to get my masters and I'm currently working on my Ph.D. Awhile back, I was a 9th grade teacher at a school in a rough area. I always wanted to go where I felt my gift could be used the most, but I noticed that most of the students were not at a comprehension level to even do the work. So I went into overdrive with after-hours programs and being more creative. Implementing systems and incentives to get them caught up but the parents complained to the school board about the work load which caused the principal to come down hard on me. The principal demanded that I lighten up on the workload and just pass the students on. I was not comfortable with this and took matters before the board myself. I lost that battle and for the first time I was lost. My whole life I knew what I wanted to do and how I was going to do it. I found myself in a place where I thought that maybe the world didn't value or even want what I had to offer. This sent me into a deep depression. I took a job at a local coffee shop just to make ends meet and was just going through the motions….but then I met Tim.

"When I met, Tim was a very high ranking member of a motor cycle gang and had just lost someone very close to him and really wanted to make some changes in his life. He started going to the library once a day for about an hour that is where we met. He would read random things just trying to figure it all out. One day he was reading a book about discovering your purpose and I noticed what he was reading and commented. "That is a very good book, but I'm not so sure that I believe what it says anymore."

Tim who was a little reluctant to respond finally said, "Oh yeah, what makes it good?"

I replied, "Well it goes into great detail about how to discover and obtain your purpose. It all sounds really good but I don't believe it anymore because I thought I was on that path until I hit a wall and have been trying to figure it out ever since."

Tim replied, "I don't know anything about finding your purpose but I know plenty about hitting a wall and getting back up and either going through, over, under, or around the wall, but never stopping, never accept 'no' as your fate."

When I looked at him I could just tell that he meant every single word, so I said, "I will make a deal with you if you can show me how to get up and keep fighting, I can show you how to figure out your purpose."

Tim extended his hand and replied, "Well my friend, I believe you have yourself a deal."

"From that day on we became the best of friends. And that friendship lead us here, Tim is over security and self-defense training and I'm over education. This program was designed to do far more than just improve your reading comprehension, critical thinking, and information retention skills. Together we will dig up each one of your talents, dust them off, and show you how to utilize them so that you may start reaching their full potential. This isn't just some generic school system, we will work with each of you and detail the program specifically to fit each and every one of you."

"Okay let's get started for all of you that are new today, you all have a pretty simple task but it will require one hundred percent honesty. The rest of you we will need your support and encouragement. Remember it is a lot easier to tear down a building than it is to erect one. First, I will need all of you to think about what has been the most reoccurring dream that you have had dating back as far as you can remember. For some of you it may be popping into your mind as we speak and a few of you might be drawing a blank. For those who have the answer, right it down and together we are going to crack the code of how that reoccurring dream is connected to your purpose. We will apply this information in a way that will have an extremely powerful effect on the rest of your life. If you are drawing a blank, that is okay, over the next month of dissecting what I like to call your 'original dream', it will start to come back to you and you will also gain clarity on it."

"I don't what to make this sound like such an easy task because it may be one of the hardest things you have ever done, because while we are digging up your talents that may have been buried for such a long time we will also be digging up a lot of painful memories and even a lot of heart breaking questions about why certain things were allowed to happen to you. We will all work together to provide the best answer to each and every one of those questions as well. There is one thing that we need to make absolutely clear from the very beginning; what happened to you is not your fault. Blame is a very powerful thing. The more you blame yourself about something the more you will believe all of the negative things that others have said about you, but we are also not going to blame anyone else because when we do that we are signing over our rights to the power that

God has granted us over to them. We are waiting on them to have a change of heart so that our lives can be better instead of looking to God for our provision, protection, and insight on how we should be spending our time."

One of the new girls, Roslyn, raised her hand. "I'm sorry but if we are being a hundred percent up front I think I should just let you know that I don't believe in God. I'm not sure if I ever did, but if I did, after seeing how some of the so called 'men of faith' behaved in private, I definitely don't believe! One of them visited me every week since I was 16. I would see him on TV preaching to a large audience and everything. Whatever God he claims to believe in I want no part of!" Some of the girls in the room nodded their head in agreement with her.

Ryan countered "This is all a part of the process. We are not here to force you to believe in anything. Remember the most important requirement to accomplish our goal is one hundred percent honesty. In my opinion an honest atheist can be closer to God than a lying believer who made all the right claims when people were around, but behind closed doors their actions suggest that they don't really believe in anything. Our goal is to take our destiny out of the hands of others. Even if you are not quite ready to place it into the hands of God. I believe that will come with time, but you can't let how others behave shape your identity because if you do, that dark cycle that most of you were practically born into will continue."

The question that comes up the most is why me? Why was I born into a family that did not want me? Why was I caught up in a life of sex trafficking? Why was I not loved? Why was I abused? Why was I betrayed? Why was I forsaken?" By the time he got to the last question there was not a dry eye in the room.

Ryan continued, "I struggled with how to answer that question for a long time, why me? I use to just say that God's ways are not our ways and His thoughts are beyond our thoughts but that answer would leave me feeling hollow inside. I knew that there was more to it, but just didn't know how to access it. Then one night I had a dream that was so clear I woke up rejoicing because I knew exactly what it was about. In that dream I was under ground and things were closing in on me and getting tighter. I felt like I was being crushed to death. Just when I felt like I was about to die I was lifted out of the ground and placed into this fire that probably was 1000 degrees. I saw some hay and it was instantly consumed. I saw some straw and it disappeared before my very eyes. I saw some wood and it took a while but eventually the same thing happened. I saw some silver and some expensive stones and they were not completely destroyed by the fire but the damage was to the point that they were worthless and could not be used for anything. Then I looked up and saw all of this gold and diamonds. That is when God showed me what the dream was all about. The fire did not destroy the gold and these most precious diamonds, it actually made them more valuable and even stronger by removing all of the impurities."

"You see you are that gold and those diamonds that I saw in that vision. Oh if you could have seen the way they were shining in the midst of that fire while everything else was being destroyed. You were created to withstand the heat and the pressure that would destroy most people. You were created to do so because you are going to play a role in putting an end to the very thing that you were once a victim of. What happened to you didn't destroy you or define you, it only refined you and prepared you to help slay the very monster that is affecting so many lives all over the world."

"Now I'm not trying to sale you some sort of fairy-tale. This may mean you dedicating the remainder of your life to a war that might out live you. You might not live long enough to see the total victory, but if you embrace it you will obtain a fulfillment that you will not be able to find on any other path." The entire room was still crying.

Roslyn replies "I still don't think that I believe in a God, but I want to know more about the God that you believe in, because that may be the one I choose to believe." Some of the other girls laughed in agreement.

Ryan replied, "I would love to tell you more about Him, but remember no pressure, honesty is very important. When you are ready to make the decision to believe, do it for you and because you are beginning to recognize God speaking to your spirit. Not to fit in, not for me, or for anyone else. Only for you."

Alexandria another new addition raised her hand with excitement and asked "Can I go first in sharing my dream?"

Ryan encouraged her "Sure come right up and face the audience I will sit in your seat.

Everyone laughs because Ryan could barely fit.

Alexandria begins, "My reoccurring dream since I was five years old has been me as a super hero, but I was never able to fly or didn't have any special costume. I would blend in with everyone else. I had a super sense that would alert me whenever a child was in trouble. I would get there almost instantly and I had this weapon that was a very long whip with electricity going through it. I would wrap it around whoever was hurting the child. The electricity was so strong that it would leave them unconscious for a while. Sometimes I have to revisit the same houses but eventually the abuse would stop all together because they knew that if it didn't I would continue to show up. I could never forget the look on the face of the kid as I was leaving. I was never able to say anything for some reason, but whenever they would look at me it was as if they were starring at an angel or something. (Alexandria dropped her head) I know that sounds crazy right?"

Ryan didn't even let her finish, "No not at all. As a matter of fact, your dream is pretty easy to crack. I will get with you and Tina. We are going to get started on the education portion as soon as we can get the details worked out. You are going to be one of the best psychologist and social workers the world has ever seen. Alexandria laughed with this shy excitement and everyone else cheered for her.

Roslyn waves her hand like it is an emergency. "I want to go next!"

Ryan replied, "Go right ahead, Alexandria sit in her seat your seat is kind of full at the moment." Everyone laughed.

Roslyn begin, "Ever since I was young I would always have this dream were I could see when someone was sick. The sickness would show up as a different color on their body. All I had to do was be bold enough to walk up to them and touch the area where I saw the different color and a warm glow would come from my hand. I could see the color leave their body. When this happened, you could see on their faces that they were getting better. I would go all over the world but mostly to places that had a lot of people that could not afford to go to doctors and hospitals. Whenever I would touch them and make them better they would get so happy and that would make me happy!" She gave the biggest smile and everyone clapped for her.

Ryan responded with a serious look on his face, "Huh, I sensed that about you the day you got here. You are a healer. I will get with you and Ms. Elizabeth. Did you know that she is a retired nurse practitioner? If you stick with this you will have the word Doctor in front of your name before you know it. You will have the education and the credentials to go along with your gift. The same way you saw yourself in your dream going all over the world healing people is actually what is going to happen. It will be a long road through medical school, residency, and dealing with all of the naysayers who won't understand your gift, but they can't take away your 'original dream', not if you don't let them. The only person that can stop it is you." Everyone cheered again. "Okay that is all the time that we have for today." The room voiced their disappointment. "But remember no matter how crazy or far-fetched that reoccurring dream may sound to you, if you are brave enough to stand before us and share it we will do whatever it takes to crack that code and set you on the path to greatness!"

After class, I headed to a nearby oak tree where Kevin's tombstone was next to Annabelle's. I kneeled next to Kevin's and put some fresh flowers on their tombstones.

"Now I am starting to see the words that you spoke that night coming to life. God has place something inside me that allowed me to survive the worst while he was preparing me for the best. My inner beauty not only helped me to understand who God was and the major role that He would play in my life, but also who I am and the major role I was created to carry on while on earth. Walking down this divine path toward my destiny gives me this high that I can't even put into words. I want to help as many girls as possible to experience this high. I'm still baffled by how one question could make such a difference in me. The first time you asked me to tell you why I'm beautiful I thought that you were crazy, but little by little it started to awaken something on the inside of me. We will do our best to do that for every girl here."

I closed my eyes and thought about Kevin and what he did for me.

"I wish you could be here and see all that we have accomplished because of you!" I said to him and somehow I knew he could hear me. "You heard the gun shot but you still came to save me. For that, and the rest that you have done for me, I am more thankful for you than I have been for anything else in my life."

I opened my eyes and tears started falling to the grass.

I got up and went back to the house. There were a lot of things to take care before the end of the day and one of them was the girl's dinner. I used to help Elizabeth prepare dinner because it was an opportunity to draw from her wisdom. She was by far the wisest person that I had ever met.

Every evening after the girls had dinner I used to sit at the table with Elizabeth and discuss things…and that night was no exception.

"Did Judith enjoy her first day?" Elizabeth asked me as we were sitting at the kitchen table.

"She did actually, I even saw her smiling a few times!" I replied and Elizabeth smiled.

"That's great news, once they realize they've got a second chance at life, they will see things with different eyes!"

"I had a nice heart to heart with Kevin today." I confessed to Elizabeth.

"I'm sure he listened and smiled down on you!" She added, "He loved you so much!"

"I know." I replied, "My life started when I met you two…what happened before that…was all just preparation."

She reached across the table and grabbed my hands, Elizabeth had a kind motherly look on her face and this warmed my heart… every time.

"Without your experiences and courage, I'm not sure if what we are witnessing right now would even be possible, these girls are being reborn!" she said to me. So much truth was coming out of her mouth.

"You're right!" I replied and thought about Judith. "I'm going to check on Judith, I know how hard the first nights can be."

"You do that, but you need to rest too…you're working yourself too hard." she said to me with the kind voice of a concerned mother.

"Yes mom, I'll do just that." I replied, kissed her hand and went upstairs to see what Judith was doing.

Chapter 9

Preparing for the worst

I QUIETLY OPENED THE DOOR TO JUDITH'S ROOM, AND peaked in to see if she was sleeping. She seemed asleep but right as I was about to close the door I saw this small red light coming from Judith's silver bracelet. I had seen it on her wrist before but thought nothing of it.

I did not do anything at that moment because I did not want to wake her up. In the morning I called Tina, Tim, and Ryan for a meeting because I wanted to discuss the bracelet.

"I'm worried about this bracelet of hers...something is off, I'm telling you!" I said and Tina downplayed it.

"Maybe it's just some fashion thing..." she replied.

"I doubt that, bracelets don't just blink like that. It has to have some sort of electronic device attached to it!" Tim argued and I agree with him.

"This can be some sort of tracking device...we need to take a better look at it!" I said.

"It's not like she's a dog or something..." Tina tried to defend her cause, but I knew better.

"Tina...stop that!" I said.

"I'm sorry...I guess anything is possible these days, I just think that it's too much..." she said.

Judith was coming down the stairs right when we were in the middle of our discussion.

"Judith, honey? Could you come down here for a moment please?" I asked her and she gladly agreed.

She nodded "Is everything ok?"

"Yes of course" I replied trying not to startle her. "Just wanted to know how you're feeling?"

"Great" she replied smiling "I don't think I have slept like that since I was a baby..."

We all started laughing.

"Judith, do you mind if Tim takes a look at your bracelet while you are eating breakfast?" I asked as the laughing ended.

"Why?" she asked confused and I just had to come clean.

"Well..." I tried to confess but Tim stepped in.

"I have this great technique that will make it shine even brighter than when it was new" he said and Judith agreed.

"I guess that's ok!"

She took it off gently and placed it on Tim's hands.

"Just be careful with it ok?" Judith added with a concerned voice.

"I promise I will!" Tim said to her.

"Now enjoy your breakfast!" I said and smiled at her.

Judith left and we began to investigate the mystery of the blinking bracelet. Tim put it on the table then grabbed his shoe and slammed the blinking light with the heel...and then he hit it again!

"You promised not to ruin it!" I said to him but it looked like there was no other way.

"Odds are that she will not want it back once she knows what it truly is. Trust me!" he replied and slammed it again.

A chip fell off with one of the jewels.

"It's a chip!" Tim said concerned.

"You sure?" I insisted because I did not want to make a fuss for no reason.

"Positive. We need to get the girls out of here!" he exclaimed as he rose quickly to his feet.

Tina looked like she was about to faint… "Ohh God no!!" she exclaimed. "We can say we are going on a field trip!"

"We gotta get moving!" Tim insisted and right then we a heard knock on the door! Our hearts froze thinking the worst.

"Oh no." I whispered.

"Can someone get that for me?" Elizabeth said from the kitchen.

"I'll get it." Tim offered and made signals to us that we should prepare the girls. "Get them out of here!" he whispered.

We had no idea how or where we should take them. Tina looked at me confused…

"We don't have a bus and we can't fit them all in our cars!"

I was so scared and feared that an army of pimps were at the door looking for their girls, but when Tim opened the door, he could not see anyone. The porch was empty.

"No one there!" he said and returned into the house.

This was weird, but I could feel that something bad was about to happen. That bracelet could lead Judith's father or whoever was tracking her straight to our door. It was time to move!

We gathered all the girls in the kitchen as we decided to leave through the back door. Elizabeth was there as usual doing her business, cooking and cleaning for the girls and she sensed that something was wrong.

"What's going on?" she asked but I could not tell her the truth.

"Nothing" I replied "Just taking the girls out for a bit…Come on girls."

Elizabeth gave me a look of wonder, which I tried to avoid.

"Are we doing self-defense early today?" one of the girls asked and I nodded positively.

"Should I be concerned?" Elizabeth insisted and I did not know what lie to tell this time.

"Not yet" I replied and opened the door with my back as I was looking at Elizabeth. I did not see what waited for us outside.

I only realized when Judith said "Dad?!" with fear and her body started trembling.

As I turned my head I was shocked at what I saw.

Francisco was standing there in front of me…smiling. Francisco's smile suddenly turned into shock when he saw that both Tina and I were there…alive.

"Oh no…" Tina's voice trembled with fear.

"Jaime…Tina…you're both alive! Oh my God, I never thought I would see you again!" Francisco said and walked up to me. My knees got weak for a moment and I guess he felt that. He came and brushed his hand against my face, feeling my scars.

Tim was not aware of the fact that Francisco was at the back door, and when he finally got there, he didn't wait a second before he pulled out his gun aiming at Francisco's head.

"Get your hands off of her!" Tim yelled at him.

Tim's voice helped me snap out of my trance and I backed a few steps away from Francisco who was still standing there. The girls got scared and moved close to each other all looking at Tim and Francisco.

Even with the gun pointed directly at his head, Francisco did not look one bit nervous. He had seen too much in his life to be sacred by a gun threat.

"So you're the ones stealing the girls all this time" he said shaking his head. "I should have known."

I could feel my body temperature rise as the anger began to build inside of me.

"All of these girls were yours?" I asked him still in shock. "You animal!"

"Let's not get ugly," he replied arrogantly "just Judith, I have no business with the others!"

Judith came close to me…

"How did you find me?" she asked her father.

Tim stepped in before Francisco could say anything.

"The gift he gave you, that bracelet was a tracking device and that's how he got here!"

Judith looked disappointed at Francisco... almost crying.

"After all this time, the one nice thing you ever gave me was a trap. The only thing that had meaning to me...I can't believe you! You have no idea how much I hate you right now!" she said to him, but Francisco did not look like he cared about it at all.

Instead, he looked at me...

"You've upset a lot of powerful people by taking these girls away."

"Do I look like I care about those "powerful people"?! You are not taking them back...not as long as I'm standing here breathing!" I shouted at him and he made a facial expression as if he was willing to put an end to that breathing in order to take the girls.

Tim started losing it and got closer to Francisco pointing the gun at his forehead.

"I suggest you leave and never come back, before things get real nasty!" he said but Francisco insisted in taking Judith with him.

"I won't leave without my daughter." he replied but I kept shaking my head.

"She was never your daughter!" I yelled at him "Leave now!"

"You heard the lady!" Tim added and cocked the gun.

Francisco did not even blink and kept looking at me.

"You've grown into such a fine lady Jaime; I can't tell you how happy I am that you're alive...I prayed for your soul after that night!"

"I said leave!" Tim yelled for the last time and was about to pull the trigger.

"Ok...no need for violence!" Francisco replied and made a few steps back. "I'll go peacefully now. Goodbye Tina...Jaime...Goodbye Judith."

Judith did not even want to look at her father, so she looked away and walked back to the other girls. There was something in his attitude that made me believe that this was not going to be the end of it.

I called his name.

"Francisco!" and he turned around looking at me.

"Don't you ever show your face here again...or else you'll be dealing with me!"

He did not say anything but smiled as he turned and walked away…I went back inside and slammed the door.

Tim walked up to me.

"Are you ok?" he asked me but I wasn't…I could not be after Francisco discovered where we were living.

"I'm fine…" I replied because I did not want to create an even bigger scene. I had to be strong and help keep the girls calm.

"Is everyone ok?" I asked the girls and they all nodded yes. Things were very tense. Judith was the one who took it the hardest, so I walked up to her and hugged her.

"He's gone…you don't have to be scared." I whispered in her ear but she could not calm down.

"He'll come for me…now that he knows where I am, He won't rest until he gets me back!" she replied almost crying.

I searched for words of comfort to reassure her that nothing like that would ever happen. "He'll do no such thing!" I replied. I could feel all of the girls looking at us.

There was a dark cloud of fear in the house now and everyone was wondering if or when Francisco would come back. After dinner was served and all the girls were sent to their rooms, we sat around the table in the living room. Myself, Tina, Tim, Ryan and Elizabeth. We needed to come up with a plan to get the girls out of harm's way.

"I think the best thing to do now is for us to move somewhere else." I said and they looked at me. "Francisco knows that we're alive and also that his daughter is with us."

They all shook their heads approving my idea.

"We need to get out of here right away! I am afraid to spend another night here…the safety I felt for so long is all gone, I'm scared that he'll come back sooner than we expect." said Tina but we did not have anywhere to go so suddenly.

"We can't leave tonight!" I replied "We don't even have a plan, and even if we get enough vehicles we can't start driving aimlessly, the girls will be terrified!"

"I don't think that is an issue anymore." Tim intervened "We need to come up with something and we need to do it fast."

"Fine" I agreed "The first ` thing in the morning we'll talk to them and find the best solution."

"As for tonight, I'll stay up and keep watch." Tim said. "I've already put out a call to a few buddies to prepare for the worse. No one is getting in this house!"

Elizabeth was nervous. She never really dealt with this world…of pimps, guns and violence.

"Shouldn't we call the police?" she asked.

"The cops will not help us in any way" I replied. I knew better… Francisco was connected to all the high level officials in the city and state, the police department was no exception.

"But they are paid to protect us!" Elizabeth said looking worried and confused.

"Liz, we pay them with tax dollars but Francisco and his associates pay them with cash" I replied. She looked shocked but understood.

"Somehow, I knew this moment would come…I could feel it, like a shadow that never completely left." I said.

We all shared that same desolated face. It looked like our efforts over the years had been in vain and all because of a bracelet. Our future and the future of the girls was shadowed by uncertainty.

"Why don't you girls get some rest…I'll stay up and watch the house!" Tim broke the silence.

"Thank you Tim" I replied and he smiled slightly.

We left the room and went upstairs to try to rest. I checked on Judith to see if she was sleeping and she was indeed. I closed the door slowly and went into my room; I was tired and feeling defeated, and I fell asleep as soon as I laid my head on the

Chapter 10

Unforgettable Night

ANASTY NIGHTMARE TOOK OVER MY MIND AS I WAS
asleep. Francisco somehow had taken all the girls from us and forced
them onto the streets again. He also kept Tina and I as hostages to
witness how he was tormenting them. Everything seemed so real
and after a while, I opened my eyes breathing heavily. My heart was
pounding in my chest, it seemed so loud but then I thought I heard
something. I looked to the door but it was still closed.

"Phew… only a dream" I thought to myself and tried to get back
to sleep. Right as I was about to turn on the other side, I felt heavy
breathing in the back on my head.

"You were always so beautiful." Francisco whispered.

He covered my mouth with his hand to prevent me from screaming. I
tried to bite his hand, but it had no effect on him. He was laughing quietly.

When I tried to grab his hand, I felt the cold barrel of his gun
stick to my temple.

"If you make a sound, you're dead!" he said to me and then let me go.

He pulled back his gun but it was still pointed at me. I noticed
that he was holding Tim's gun. My eyes widened, as my first thought
was that he had killed him.

"Did you kill him?" I said.

He nodded no…"He's just passed out, don't worry…he'll be fine…probably." he replied and put that classic smirk back on his face.

I got up from the bed with the gun still pointed at my head. I kept thinking that all the lives in the house were in my hands now and the wrong move could turn into a bloody catastrophe.

As he leaned towards me, I tried to get as far away as possible from him.

"Stay away from me." I eventually said, as he did not stop.

"Didn't you hear me?" I insisted.

Francisco stopped right there in the middle of the room…and looked at me standing under the moonlight shining through the window.

"You still don't know me…after all these years, you think I would hurt you? Remember that I killed Bob for what he did to you…and he was like family to me!" Francisco said trying to appeal to my emotions.

I was not going to fall for his theatrical act… not after all the things he allowed to happen to me over the years.

"You hurt me in so many ways, even if you were never the one to do it yourself, you allowed Bob and a countless number of men to brutalize me over and over again." I replied but he kept going on with his monologue.

"Let's start over." he said with a serious face. Still, I was not buying into it.

"Ha…start over?" I laughed, "You act as if we had some sort of loving relationship…you're wasting your time." I said to him and ran to the corner of the room, the one next to the window.

"Is that how it is… after all those years, after all that I have done for you, all the nice things that I bought for you?" he tried to persuade me.

"It was a living hell for me!" I replied acidly and I could see that he was turning towards his 'dark side'. Francisco was not a man to take no for an answer.

When he started biting his lower lip it meant that he was about to do lose it. I had to be prepared no matter what…but at the same time I had to keep him distracted somehow.

"I don't ever want to see your face again…and I have no intention of going back with you to that sick world of yours. You hear me? I'd rather die than be your slave again!"

"When were you my slave?" he asked rhetorically.

"You know better…and that's why I hate you!"

"There's no need for such harsh words…I always thought that I treated you well. I was fair. I provided a beautiful life for you and in return, you worked for me." he replied and I was beyond disgusted by his words.

"A beautiful life you say? You made me sleep with strangers so you could afford a lavish house and lifestyle and you call that fair?" I almost shouted at him "We have different definitions of fairness… trust me on that!"

It was clear to me that Francisco did not like what he was hearing, and with every word I said, he was getting closer and closer. I turned my head toward the window wondering if I could escape through it and just then I saw a letter opener in the casing on the window…I was too far to grab it, so I waited for the perfect moment.

"I can make you change your mind you now…treat you better…" he said, and I listened to him and kept this game going just so I could buy more time.

"You're never going to stop coming after us, are you? Even if we manage to get away this time, you will not rest until you find us again!"

He smiled slightly… and shook his head to the side.

"You see," he said in a cocky voice, "when your property gets stolen, you tend to do whatever it takes to get it back…especially when it's valuable to you. I don't know if you understand my point…but…"

"So that's what you considered me, for all those years…your property!" I replied and he rushed to correct me.

"Of course not… you meant a lot more to me, and you know that…I was just speaking the truth here. I've always hated cowards and liars!" he insisted.

"I'm your friend…you should always keep that in mind. I did not come here to hurt you, or any of the girls…not even that prick you had on the couch waiting for me! He was sleeping when he was supposed to protect you…one hell of a man!" he added and I got pretty pissed off.

"I don't know why you regard me as a monster…I am a human being just like you with a past similar to yours. I have feelings…love, hate…you name it…but you don't really know me."

"Enlighten me then!" I replied sarcastically.

"I never knew my father. When I was about fourteen my mom started working for a pimp we called Big Mike. At the time she thought it would be the quickest way to better life for me and my sister. Well, she died when I was 17, they had her cremated and put her ashes in some used urn. My sister was two years younger than me. The only thing that was stopping Big Mike from making me and my sister work for him was my mom. The day she died he came looking for us. I wasn't about to let that happen. I refused to sleep with men or women for money and he threatened to kill me and my sister, so I killed him. I thought I was doing everybody a favor. The next day all of the girls that were working for Big Mike pleaded with me to take over for him and protect them including my baby sister. I did everything in my power to convince them that they were free and they could go and be whatever they wanted to be. Especially my baby sister, she was so smart. But they insisted that if I declined they would just go and find someone else. So finally I agreed to protect them, they would pay me to do so of course. The word quickly began to spread and before I knew it I was one of the biggest business men in the city. My baby sister became a beautiful shell stunning on the outside hollow on the inside. A few of the pimps that were losing money to me figured out the best way to get back at me was to hit closest to my heart. So they went out and kidnapped the love of my life and my sister. They injected them with lots of heroin for weeks. My sister died instantly, as if she was ready to go, and although they released my love, she was never the same. She had become addicted and I had to watch as she declined until finally she overdosed. That pain was worse than watching my own mother slowly succumb to drugs. If I had any piece of a heart left it was taken during this process. I became numb to everything. That was a long time ago but I have never loved anyone else the way that I loved her. What you have done for yourself and are doing for these girls is something that I always dreamed about but never thought was possible. I am so proud of you."

I asked "what was her name, your love." He reached around his neck and rubbed this gold locket with his fingers. He didn't answer me but just stared off into the distance for a moment. I could tell that he was being sincere, but I also knew that he was trying to get me to let my guards down for a reason. Francisco playing that sentimental role was unnatural. He was a different kind of pimp but when the situation called for it he left his mysterious aura to the side and got hard-core.

"Now, I think I am going to put the gun down, I don't think I'm gonna need it anyway." he said and placed in on the floor next to him.

"No, you don't." I said and cheered on the inside because I knew that now I would have a chance to strike.

I had become a pro at crying over time, so I kinda controlled this as needed. I filled my eyes with tears and looked at Francisco as if I was begging for forgiveness.

"Do you still love me?" I asked him with all the sincerity I could muster.

"You know I do." he replied with a softer voice than usual. "I never stopped loving you, I thought about you often, since that night at the river."

"You know I always felt you with me…I don't know why or how but I just knew you were there." I replied with a sensual voice and managed to get into his mind.

"Jaime…your words touch my heart." he said and came close, in breathing range. I could feel him breathing heavily in my face and I could even feel his heart beat. His heart was racing and I knew that I only had one chance, if I missed I was done!

His fingers softly traced the course of my scars. He looked like he was admiring the marks I had on my face…as if they were some kind of living work of art.

"I give you my word…from now on, no one will ever hurt you again. You can trust me." he whispered in my ear and then kissed my cheek.

"I know that." I replied and pulled to the side a little bit, closer to the window.

He smiled at me…

I knew it was now or never, so I had to distract his attention somehow. I grabbed his waist with my left hand and drew him closer to me…

"You know…" I kissed his cheek and could feel his body begin to slightly relax.

I took advantage of the moment, grabbed the letter opener with my right hand and stabbed him in the neck! Blood started flowing everywhere. "…you're the worst liar ever!" I finished my sentence and pushed him away from me.

He was bleeding heavily as I struck the main artery in his neck. He tried desperately to grip the letter opener and pull it out, but it was in vain…he could not grasp it with all the blood. When he finally managed to pull the opener out, the hole in his neck left blood gushing out. I just stood there and watched as breathing became more and more difficult for him.

"You're no different than Big Mike…may God have mercy on your soul!"

He started blinking rapidly and spit up blood a few times. A pool of blood grew around him. All of a sudden I started to feel really sorry for him and regretted what I had just done. I thought about his story and realized that he was a part of the same vicious cycle. He didn't start out as a monster he started out wanting to protect himself and his family from the monster. His life was marked for destruction before it really got started. What have I just done, this man treated me better than my birth mother and father ever did? In that moment

I felt lost, the magnitude of my actions coupled with how massive this sex trafficking problem really is hit me like a ton of bricks.

As he was lying on the floor, I noticed him gripping the golden locket he was rubbing earlier. I had seen it before, and it looked like he never took it off. I never dared to ask him about it and it wasn't my business really, but now curiosity got the best of me. I had to know. I opened it and almost fainted at what I saw!

"God, it can't be!" I said to myself but the resemblance was uncanny. I realized that Annabelle and his love were one and the same! For all those years Kevin and Elizabeth had no idea about the circumstances in which their daughter died...

"Oh, God, what have I done?" I said to myself but I quickly remembered that everyone at the ranch was in danger. So I made a choice and it is one that I will have to live with for the rest of my life.

It might sound weird or twisted but I felt like he needed to be buried next to Annabelle. So I ran downstairs and woke Tim up. "Tim...Tim...wake up!" I started his body. He smelled like alcohol had been poured on his face...but I soon realized that this was the way Francisco managed to knock him out.

Tim eventually woke up, dizzy and with a weird expression on his face.

"Your covered in blood!" he exclaimed and jumped off the sofa.

"I know!" I replied "I don't have time to explain, come with me!"

Tim followed me upstairs where he saw Francisco lying in a bloodbath.

I grabbed the sheets off the bed and helped to wrap his body.

Tim didn't say a word, he just picked up his body and started carrying him outside.

"I think that we should bury him next to Annabelle I will explain later, the girls must not know about this!" I replied.

While Tim was digging the hole I was inside cleaning up all the blood. It all took place in perfect silence. By the time Tim was finished digging the hole I was back out there to help. We threw his body in and began filling the hole. The next day I planted some beautiful flowers over it to cut down on any possible questions.

"Since that night Tim and I have never brought it up and I have never spoken a word about it until today."

"Each day that I wake up in the morning, everything I do and everything I think about is geared toward helping these girls unlock there inner beauty so they can go on to accomplish amazing things in their life.

Back at the university

"For the first time since that night I have decided to face my greatest fear of revealing my darkest secret. I'm willing to face whatever consequences may follow this decision. This is something that I had to do for me, but I'm also doing it for someone in the audience who needs to know that you are beautiful in ways that can't be described with words and that there are people out there that love you and will risk their life to protect you."

"This is my story, for better or worse."

All the students were standing up applauding and crying. I thanked everyone, bowed a couple of times and turned to the left where Tina is waiting for me smiling. I smiled back and then turned and thanked my extraordinary audience again before walking off the stage.

"You were amazing up there. Jaime, thank you." Tina whispers to me and I nodded because I knew why she was thanking me. She never knew what happened to Francisco only Tim and I did.

In the hallway, some of the students approach me. The looks on their faces said it all…

"Hi Jaime, my name is Rachel and I have to confess that your story…it really stuck with me, I am impressed of how strong you were and still are to go out there and tell the world your truth!"

"I'm glad to hear that." I reply smiling. "I had to go out there so that the whole world hears about my story and the story of so many other girls!"

"I really needed to hear that, more than you know!" Rachel adds and I look at Tina with concern.

"Are you okay?" I asked her.

"Well," Rachel says, "I've never really been in your situation but… but…my father…used to molest me for years."

"Oh my God," I exclaimed "you poor soul!"

"Yeah I know…I was scared of him for so long! Eventually I worked up the courage to say something and now he is in jail."

"You did the right thing!" I encouraged her, but she still had this scared look on her face.

"I know," she replies "but I heard that my dad's lawyer pulled some strings and he's due to leave the prison in about a week. I am afraid that he'll come looking for me and I don't know what's going to happen to me if he manages to find me!"

Rachel starts crying right there in front of me and I could see that she is absolutely terrified by the monster that was her own father.

I hug her and brush her hair off her forehead.

"You know you can come to us if you're in need of protection. Our arms are always open to anyone who needs help!" I said to her and her eyes widen suddenly.

"Thank you so much" she sobs "I was so scared and wanted to kill myself because I did not know where to go; he has a lot of friends in high places!" She gasps, "I'm so lucky I found you!"

"Don't worry hun, we're here to help. You don't have to worry about a thing!" I said to her and she looks up at me.

"Are you sure that I am not a burden?"

"Darling, don't stress yourself…whenever you're ready, we're just a phone call away. We have room at the ranch and we'll be more than happy to have you."

"Thank you so much…I just don't have the words to express my gratitude." she smiles at me and I could see the hope in her eyes.

"Plus, we added a new wing to the ranch with tons of comfy rooms that need people to live in them…you'll feel right at home, trust me!" Tina adds igniting Rachel's imagination.

"You won't even know I'm there…just for a little while until the coast is clear then I'll come back." she said timidly.

"There is a thing though" I said to her with a straight face and she looks at me rather puzzled "Before you leave, you have to tell us why you're beautiful. There is no precise answer…we just need to hear it coming from you."

She looks at me and smiles widely.

"I'll do the best I can" and jumps in my arms. We hug, all three of us in a clump of happiness. As we were hugging I looked up and noticed an officer standing there. He had a very serious look on his face. He waited until we finished embracing then said, "We need to talk."

The End

Conclusion

ABOUT 40% OF AMERICAN PROSTITUTES WERE FORMER child prostitutes forced into prostitution. 60% of children reported missing as a result of running away become prostitutes for some period of time. The average age at which a prostitute begins their illegal work is 14 years old. 58% of American prostitutes reported violent assault at the hands of their clients or their pimps. As we assist our young woman in unlocking their inner beauty and discovering who they were created to be, we